"You really like this, don't you?" Mark shouted above the sound of the glowing furnaces.

Sharon laughed in answer, her pulse racing with excitement. "It's glorious!" she called back. "So much raw power!"

"Well," he said more softly, "under that cool, professional exterior a warm heart doth really beat. Just like it used to."

Sharon let her eyes meet his. She felt a crackle of heat in her own body, as though one of the sparks that still jumped occasionally from the furnace had come too close. Mark reached toward her, and Sharon knew he must have felt that abrupt, fiery explosion, too. With one hand he tipped the hard hat off her head, and he slid his other hand beneath the jacket of her suit, encircling her waist and pulling her hard against him. Dizzying warmth billowed up within her as she closed her eyes and opened her mouth to his . . .

Dear Reader:

Spring is here! And we've got six new SECOND CHANCE AT LOVE romances to add to your pleasure in the new season. So sit back, put your feet up, and enjoy . . .

You've also got a lot to look forward to in the months ahead—delightful romances from exciting new writers, as well as fabulous stories from your tried-and-true favorites. You know you can rely on SECOND CHANCE AT LOVE to provide the kind of satisfying romantic entertainment you expect.

We continue to receive and enjoy your letters—so please keep them coming! Remember: Your thoughts and feelings about SECOND CHANCE AT LOVE books are what enable us to publish the kind of romances you not only enjoy reading once, but also keep in a special place and read again and again.

Warm wishes for a beautiful spring.

Ellen Edwards

Ellen Edwards
SECOND CHANCE AT LOVE
The Berkley Publishing Group
200 Madison Avenue
New York, N.Y. 10016

NIGHT FLAME

SARAH CREWE

SECOND CHANCE AT LOVE
BOOK

With special thanks to Murray Small

Other Second Chance at Love books by
Sarah Crewe

GOLDEN ILLUSIONS   #135

Second Chance at Love books are published by
The Berkley Publishing Group
200 Madison Avenue, New York, NY 10016

*For my mother and father
and for Joanie,
without any of whom
this book would not exist.*

Chapter 1

SHARON DYSART REACHED the crest of the last hill and smiled. The Otawnee River Valley stretched out before her in the night, and at its center, just as she remembered, lay the Number One mill of SomerSteel. The fires of the great furnaces lent a soft orange glow to the sky all around, and, with the car windows open to the July heat, Sharon could hear the muffled hissing of hot metal being poured, like some faraway giant drawing deep breaths.

Impulsively she stepped on the accelerator and headed down the hill, drawn like a moth to the fires of the mill. No security guard moved out to stop her at the gate, so she drove into the dark lot and pulled her rented car into an open space. She could smell it now, too—the acrid odor of the blast furnace and of steel being rolled out— and she was amused to feel her pulse quicken slightly. "After all these years," she murmured wryly, "and all these steel mills."

Once out of the car, Sharon picked her way carefully around piles of scrap metal and slab steel to a shed so huge it could have covered ten football fields. Through an opening in one side she could see a slab of steel, reheated to a glowing red-orange, moving steadily back and forth along the yard-wide track of the hot strip mill. Rollers above and below would shape it, lengthen it; eventually it would be hundreds of feet long and only a fraction of an inch thick.

The process hadn't changed much since she had watched it as a child at this very same mill. Twenty-odd years ago she had listened raptly as her father explained his job here. Sharon could remember standing in almost this same place, feeling the heat of the strip and the moist steam it formed as the cooling water hit it, hearing the hissing and the metallic clashes. And she could remember her father's hand on her shoulder. With a little sigh, she turned away.

Now she taught mill owners how to get rid of the massive, awkward, and sometimes unsafe equipment and replace it with more modern, computer-controlled technology. But part of her regretted the loss. She loved the way it all felt: the heat and the sounds, the sense that invisible giants were at work in the darkness, that dwarf-like men only carried out their orders.

She ran a hand through her thick black hair. It felt gritty and in need of a wash after the long, hot day's drive. With a wide yawn, she headed back toward her car.

A man was leaning against the driver's side. She couldn't discern much about him in the glow of the single, unshielded bulb lighting that part of the lot. The rim of his hard hat threw a shadow across his face, but the outline of his tall, rangy body was clear. He wore overalls and a T-shirt.

Sharon slowed her pace a little and glanced around the parking lot. There was no one else in sight. She grasped her shoulder bag with one hand and wrapped the other tightly around her car keys.

"This is private property, lady," the man said as she approached. His voice was deep and cheerfully lazy, but he kept one elbow on the roof of her car.

"I'm aware of that," she began politely, smiling a little and squinting at his face, still unable to make out his features in the darkness. "I'll be—"

"We don't get a lot of female company around here in the middle of the night," he interrupted. He sounded amiable, almost flirtatious. It was not a tone Sharon was precisely in the mood for. "Except we do get the occasional lady looking for work. You know the kind of lady. The kind who works at night."

Sharon could see a sudden gleam of white teeth as he grinned at her. She blinked in disbelief, then smiled grimly. "I *will* be working, thank you," she said. "Here. And if you want to keep *your* job, I'd suggest you get out of my way and let me out of here. If you're paid to stop people like me at the gate, your boss might be interested in knowing just where you were when I drove in."

"You'll be working *here,* will you?" Suddenly the man switched on a flashlight and shone it directly at her. Sharon instinctively raised her hand to shield her eyes from the industrial-strength beam. She glared in his direction, but he had virtually disappeared behind the blinding light.

"My, my," the man's voice said from the darkness. It sounded interested now. "Very nice, indeed." There was a short silence, as though he were carefully studying her. "But no ID," he abruptly added, "and that means no job here. On your way."

Sharon reached out and pushed the light to one side.

"There's nothing I'd like more than to be on my way, believe me. But you're making that a little difficult." She gestured at his arm, which still blocked her access to the car.

He dropped his hand to his side with a little mock bow. Sharon could see by the light of the flashlight that he was grinning again, his teeth white against the shadows of his face. With a brisk nod she stepped by him, pulled open the driver's door, and slipped into the car.

The man swung the door shut behind her. Then, as she started the car, he leaned forward slightly, resting one hand on the lowered window. The flashlight still dangled from his other hand. For the first time since he had appeared in the darkness, Sharon got a clear look at his face in the soft light from her dashboard, and she swallowed hard as her eyes and brain registered his features: a high, broad forehead; light-colored eyes set deep beneath thick brows that also looked light; a slightly crooked nose; a firm chin. The hard hat covered his hair except for a few little twists that escaped beneath it. Longish, it would seem, and curly.

Sharon felt a sudden tingling in her fingertips. It was an impressive face—elegant, sharp-featured, but amused as well. And there was something, she thought suddenly, vaguely familiar about it. A tiny pulse began to beat at the side of her throat.

"By the way," the man said, still smiling, "it isn't exactly my regular job, stopping people at the gate. But if you really want to report me to someone, I guess you should try old Byron Somers. My name's Somers, too. Mark Somers."

The pulse in Sharon's throat turned into a hammer blow as Mark Somers bowed, waved, and, with a few quick steps, disappeared into the darkness. Sharon stared at the place he had been as a knot slowly formed in her stomach. Then, with a muttered word of the sort she rarely used, she shoved the car into gear and stamped on the accelerator.

Mark Somers. Of course. Leave it to me, she thought angrily, to pick a fight with Mark Somers the first hour I'm in town. The car banged across the railroad tracks, and Sharon wound her way back up the hill through the city of Somerville. She made the turns almost automatically; fifteen years away hadn't made much difference in the layout of the place.

But they've made a whole lot of difference in me, she told herself, trying to make the anger cool, trying to escape the picture of a handsome, unlined face, a face fifteen years younger than the one she'd glimpsed tonight. She slammed one hand against the steering wheel, willing the image out of her head. It was odd she hadn't recognized him, she thought as she reached the top of the hill and turned into the wide front driveway of the Otawnee Inn. There had been a brief time when that face had been the most important one in the world for her.

She smiled as she angled the car into a parking space. Maybe not so odd, after all. One hardly expected to find the mill owner's son running around in overalls at ten o'clock at night, filling in for the security guard.

Sharon glanced up at the elegant, white-shuttered, brick facade of the inn as she slid out of the car and unlocked the trunk. The house she had grown up in, across the river in Otawnee, had been sold at the time of her father's death twelve years ago, and that had been the last time she had set foot in the Otawnee Valley.

The offer of a three-week consulting contract with SomerSteel had come at a time when she had nothing on her immediate schedule, and she had agonized over it briefly. Then, when she had accepted it, she had decided to treat herself to a stay at the Otawnee Inn—the symbol, during her childhood, of the Somers family and their world. A place she had only visited once, for her high school graduation dinner with her father.

She smiled wryly at the memory. It had not been a success. They had struggled with the French menu, and her father had been distinctly uncomfortable. But now . . . well, French menus were hardly an obstacle after seven years in Paris.

A bellman, looking vaguely unhappy in Williamsburg knickers and wig, had materialized next to her. She handed him the leather suitcase and garment bag from the trunk and left the microcomputer for morning. *This* time, she told herself as she followed the man up the broad front steps of the inn, this time even old Byron Somers himself can see I belong here.

When her travel alarm shattered the silence the next morning at six-thirty, Sharon was already awake. Sleep had been long in coming and, when it finally arrived, had been punctuated by dreams that made it restless. Images she had buried deep beneath other memories had floated in the darkness: the confident, almost arrogant, face of Mark Somers smiling out from the newspaper after a family trip somewhere exotic; Mark smiling at her—miraculously, at *her!*—from the side of the basketball court. Finally Sharon had lain awake, keeping the images away with the help of a steel-making journal.

She reached over to turn off the jangling alarm. She knew she could probably sleepwalk through the day. First days on a job were always pretty much the same, and she had used a lot of energy in trying to convince herself that this one was no more important than any other. She went through her usual discipline of laying out the schedule in her head: breakfast here at the inn with Byron Somers, chairman of SomerSteel; a tour of the mill— this time with proper identification; lunch with Byron and the other senior officers; then down to work.

But she stared at the ceiling as she ticked off the meetings. There was no getting around it: It *was* more important here. It was home. She wanted it to be perfect. And Mark Somers was getting in the way. A young Mark Somers—with close-cropped, sandy-colored hair; piercing light blue eyes; a wonderful body with the broad shoulders and long, muscular legs of a runner and a basketball player. There had been a breezy confidence about him that none of Sharon's friends had had, but there had also been something beneath that—something intelligent, some hint of trouble to come—and that vague hint had fascinated her most.

She shook her head. It was Byron Somers who had requested her services, Byron with whom she had signed the contract. Mark's name had never been mentioned in the negotiations. She had hardly given Mark a second thought; she remembered having heard somewhere that he hadn't returned to Somerville after college, that he had thumbed his nose at the mill and his father's money. She wondered briefly just what he'd been doing at ten o'clock last night. Was he back? Would he be part of her job? Then she shook her head again and swung her legs over the side of the bed. "I'll cross that bridge when I come to it," she told herself with a little sigh.

After showering she dressed with her usual care and conservatism in a tan lightweight linen suit, arranged her freshly washed ebony hair into a tight twist, then hooked small gold hoops through her ears. She brushed on peach-colored blusher and surveyed the finished product in the mirror. It *was* a product, she was the first to acknowledge. She dressed to suit the needs of her job—and the desires of her employers: dignified, businesslike, neither too feminine nor too masculine. Cool.

She stuck her tongue out at the reflection. It all looked stylish; there was no doubt about that. Paris—and Jean-Paul, to give credit where it was due—had provided style. She had almost forgotten what it was like to dress in the clothes she used to love—the loose, Indian cottons—and to braid her hair down her back. With a grin and not much hope, she ran a finger over her thick, almost wild black eyebrows. They were her one indulgence—not at all in the image she so carefully cultivated, but a token sign of individuality. She adamantly refused to pluck them.

She turned away from her reflection, picked up her briefcase, tucked her wallet inside it, and headed downstairs.

A few minutes later Sharon watched Byron Somers cross the inn dining room. At almost seventy, he looked barely fifty. His tall, slender body was elegantly clad in a perfectly fitted gray suit, and his white hair was carefully cut to frame the narrow, handsome features of his face. There was a courtly look about him, but there was also a twinkle in his light blue eyes that surprised Sharon.

She rose and held out a hand as he approached the table. Byron grasped it in both of his and patted it tenderly. It was the kind of gesture she might have expected from him—and would normally have been annoyed by—but somehow he carried it off with aplomb.

"Miss Dysart! I'm delighted to see you." He smiled broadly, and Sharon's own smile tightened imperceptibly. The Somers charm in high gear, she told herself wryly.

"How do you do, Mr. Somers. It's nice to be here." She gestured vaguely around the dining room, as if including it in her pleasure.

"Ah, but you've been here before, of course. So you should say it's good to be *back*." Byron settled Sharon into her chair again and then sat down himself.

It was the stuff of politeness, she knew. He had no way of knowing that she had only set foot in the inn once before in her life, although she had grown up not more than a mile away. She let her face relax a little. "Well, yes, I am coming back, of course. But I've been away so long, the Valley certainly doesn't seem like home anymore."

Byron spread the snowy linen napkin on his lap. "Coming home is always coming home, my dear, no matter how long you stay away. I'm sure you'll find that as the days go by. Home is a special place."

Sharon shook her head politely. "This is really just another job for me, Mr. Somers. I'm afraid I really don't have a home here anymore, in any case. No relatives, no house." She shifted slightly in her chair. "And I'm not precisely from Somerville, you know. I grew up across the river, in Otawnee."

Byron waved a hand in dismissal, as if to indicate that the two towns were indistinguishable, and Sharon smiled involuntarily. Byron Somers was the last person to find Somerville and Otawnee one and the same.

"I was absolutely fascinated to find that one of the nation's most acclaimed modernization experts was from right here in the Valley!" he said. "And tell me . . ." He leaned forward slightly and folded his hands on the table. "What did your father do here? Might I have known him?"

Sharon blinked, then looked steadily at Byron for a moment. Was it possible that he had forgotten entirely? Was it possible that the name Sharon Dysart really meant nothing at all to him beyond what he had read in the professional journals? She had wondered often since he had first contacted her just what his memories might be. Suddenly it seemed possible that he had no motive in choosing her beyond wanting the best for his mill.

"My father worked in your mill," she said evenly.

Byron's eyes widened in an expression of pure delight. "Isn't that wonderful!" he cried. "Isn't that remarkable! So you're already familiar with our operation?"

Sharon nodded. "I used to come watch him work sometimes. Very much against the rules." She smiled. "This is where I learned to love steel-making."

"Well. Isn't that delightful. The kind of credentials you have—Penn State and MIT and quite remarkable recommendations—and then you know the mill as well. It's almost too good to be true!"

Sharon murmured a thank you. Byron's enthusiasm

flooded over her; she found herself holding the arms of her chair tightly, as if to keep from being swept along by it. This was the man who had put an end to his son's little dalliance with a mill-worker's daughter, and now . . . It was all, she told herself, a little too effusive to be real, and she had had too much experience with charm to be taken in by it again. Jean-Paul, heaven knew, had been charming, and so, for that matter, had been Mark Somers. Charm was something to be resisted with all one's will.

Byron asked her her preferences, ordered for them both—French toast and bacon, fresh orange juice, coffee—then handed the menus to the waitress and folded his hands on the table again.

"Well, my dear, I couldn't be happier that we were able to lure you back home. And I'm looking forward to seeing the results of your work."

Again he leaned forward slightly, and Sharon was suddenly reminded of his son, leaning on the window of her car less than twelve hours earlier. She felt a little shiver race through her body at the thought. She cleared her throat and pressed her hands together, concentrating on Byron's words.

"We've had some of the same problems that other American mills are having, of course," he was saying. "But we're less affected than most. We make specialty steels, as you know, for things like golf clubs. Even when the folks on the other side of the river can't afford cars, the folks on this side still play golf." He winked conspiratorially.

Sharon kept her smile carefully neutral, but his comment had caught her off-guard. It was, she thought, a rather empty measure of her triumph. Fifteen years ago I wasn't good enough for your son, she wanted to say, and now I'm suddenly one of you. The sort who buys golf clubs.

For the first time since she had left it, Sharon felt a flicker of affection for Otawnee and for the friends of her childhood—the ones who couldn't afford cars.

"We are in a position," Byron continued, "to implement some changes. SomerSteel's Number One mill was built in the 1950s. There have been any number of improvements in the process since then. I want you to tell us which ones we can use here."

Sharon was back on firm, familiar ground. She nodded. "It will depend on a number of factors, of course: how much space and capital you have, whether or not you want to shut down while you change over, other variables. I assume you're responsible for whatever decisions are finally made?"

It was a routine question, simply getting the lines of authority straight, but Byron shifted slightly in his chair.

"Well, I'm chairman of the board, and I own a little more than half the mill. It's always been a family operation, you know. But to be honest, my son Mark will also have to be in agreement."

Sharon felt her stomach flop over. She blinked. "You didn't mention that in the contract," she said.

Byron shook his head and smiled. "I suppose I should have," he said. "But it seemed easier not to. Mark is operations manager of Number One. And he owns the other forty-five percent of SomerSteel. It was left him by my brother, who had no children."

He hesitated a moment and twisted the wedding ring on his left hand, and suddenly he looked almost his age. "He's an awfully good manager. Very good indeed. But he's opposed to modernization. Quite against it all, in fact. Says it's a matter of principle, but I'm not quite sure just what the principle is."

Byron leaned back in his chair, looking uncharacteristically unsure of himself. Thoughts and images tumbled over themselves in Sharon's head, the same ones she'd

seen last night in her dreams: Mark Somers as a senior
in high school, playing basketball for Somerville High,
looking confident and unapproachable; and then again
two years later, home from college, sitting by the court
at a Somerville–Otawnee game, asking her out. And
Byron Somers on the front page of the local newspaper,
opening some charity drive, looking elegant and aristo-
cratic and ever so charming . . .

"I'll be honest, Miss Dysart. I don't entirely understand my son. When he was younger he didn't want
anything to do with the business, and now that he's back,
his ideas are so different."

Sharon felt a sudden twinge of sympathy for the old
man. He sounded sincerely confused—and troubled—
by his inability to fathom his son. And she knew about
fathers who couldn't understand their children; she remembered with regret the long arguments with her own
father about college, about her future—arguments that
had hurt them both.

"I'm sure—" she began, but stopped almost immediately. Her voice caught in her throat as she identified
a figure standing motionless in the doorway of the dining
room. Mark Somers was staring at her, a hint of bewilderment on his face. She had no idea how long he'd been
there.

In the morning light, Sharon could see traces of the
boy she had known years ago, but this Mark Somers was
clearly no longer a boy. His hair, still sand-colored, was
no longer close-cropped. As she had noticed the night
before, it was long and even a little wild, a tangle of
tight curls. His broad forehead, then unlined, was now
slashed by several deep creases. But his eyes, the same
glittering pale blue that she remembered, still laughed.

Mark resembled his father, but there was a fullness
to him that the older man lacked—something ripe and
intriguing and alive. His face was a ruddy tan from the

sun—a sharp contrast to his father's ivory skin—and the lines across his forehead spoke of life lived at a speed and depth Byron would never have considered. He was dressed again in work clothes—tan corduroy pants and a faded denim shirt that almost matched his eyes. Sharon couldn't imagine Byron's ever appearing in such things.

Her gaze grazed past Mark's, then returned and locked into place, as if two magnetic surfaces suddenly pulled together, their force too strong to control, inseparable except through great effort. Sharon made the effort, blinking and breaking the connection.

Byron turned to follow her gaze, and he half rose from his chair as he called a good-natured greeting to his son. "So you've tracked us down! Come join us, Mark."

Mark stood a moment longer in the doorway, his eyes still on Sharon. She could feel a warmth in her cheeks, and her stomach was momentarily uneasy. She wasn't sure what was at the root of her discomfort: her new knowledge that Mark would be a daily part of her job here—and that he would disapprove of her work—or her ambiguous memories of what he had been to her years before. She straightened her shoulders and looked back at him evenly. Not again, she told herself firmly. I'm older now, and wiser. Not again.

Finally Mark came toward them, moving with the easy grace of an athlete still in peak condition. A wide smile replaced the slightly puzzled look she had seen on his face a moment earlier.

"Hi, Dad," he said, giving his father a pat. "You didn't cover your trail well enough." Then, with a hand still resting on Byron's shoulder, he grinned down at Sharon. "Hello again," he said softly.

Sharon nodded in acknowledgment as Byron shifted his gaze to her. "Again?" he repeated, a slightly puzzled look on his face.

Sharon started to answer, but before she could, Mark

said cheerfully, "Yep. I turned the young lady out of the mill around ten o'clock last night." He grinned innocently at Sharon.

She looked back at him, wondering if he had any idea who she was. Or was he his father all over again? Did the whole thing mean so little to him that he'd forgotten all about his fling with the cheerleader from Otawnee?

"Is that so?" Byron was saying. "I hadn't realized you'd already visited our operation."

"I took a quick look around when I got in last night," Sharon replied. Her eyes remained on Mark for a brief moment, then she looked back to Byron. "I was coming in from Pittsburgh, and you know how the mill looks from the top of the Pittsburgh hill." She shrugged, letting a smile settle over her face, letting the smile imply that SomerSteel Number One was simply irresistible. She could play the charm game, too, she told herself grimly.

"By the way, Mr. Somers," she added on sudden inspiration, "there was no security on the main gate. It's none of my business, of course, but it makes good sense to use some protection." She fluttered her eyelashes just a little and sent her sweetest smile in Mark's direction.

Mark's grin remained in place, but when he spoke his tone was firm. "The daily operation of the mill is my responsibility, Miss Dysart. Not my father's. You can bring any complaints to me."

"I'll keep that in mind," Sharon said. She nodded politely, but her own smile felt abruptly stretched in place, and her mouth had gone completely dry. He had called her by name. He knew who she was. He *did* remember...

Mark nodded, and Byron looked quickly back and forth between them. "I was about to feel remiss," he said with a little chuckle, "not to have introduced you two, but I guess you did that last night. In any case, Miss Sharon Dysart, my son, Mark Somers. Mark, Miss Dysart. I've engaged Miss Dysart to give us some advice on plant modernization."

Mark had been standing by the table throughout the conversation, one hand resting on his father's shoulder. Now he withdrew the hand and took a slow step sideways, then lowered himself into a chair that had been delivered by the busboy at his arrival.

"Modernization," Mark repeated slowly, rolling the word around on his tongue. "Yes, I've read about Miss Dysart's talent for making steel mills more efficient." He leaned back in his chair, holding the edge of the table with both hands. "But you know my feelings on that issue, Dad."

"I do, I do," Byron acknowledged. He looked at Sharon and let his eyes twinkle. "It has always seemed a little odd to me that my son has managed to turn out so much more conservative than I."

"Dad . . ." Mark closed his eyes briefly, and Sharon had the sense that they had gone around on this many times before. But when he opened his eyes, his smile had returned. He looked at Sharon, studying her face as he had the night before, but as if for the first time, letting his eyes wander over her wide cheekbones and full lips, her dark green eyes and thick black brows, her black hair pulled straight back—easy to slip under a hard hat— and her long throat. He glanced at her hands where they rested on the table, and Sharon felt an impulse to clench them, which she willfully resisted.

"I suspect you'd like to see Number One by daylight, Miss Dysart," he said casually. "Can I give you a tour?"

"I can—" Sharon began, but Byron interrupted her.

"That would be wonderful, Mark," he said, beaming. "I'd be delighted if you'd cooperate on this. After all, Miss Dysart is only giving us some advice. From an educated point of view."

"Educated," Mark repeated thoughtfully. Then he laid

his hands flat on the table, palms down, and pushed himself up. Sharon was suddenly aware of those hands. Strong hands, she thought. They had always been strong. She remembered how he could wrap one around a basketball in high school . . . and how he had held her the one night they had gone dancing. She stared at their tanned backs and the soft down of golden hair, at their broad, short nails with distinctive white moons. Then she blinked and shook her head.

When she looked up again he was grinning down at her, his teeth white against his tanned face.

"When you're ready, Miss Dysart," he said.

Sharon patted her mouth with her napkin and folded it by her empty plate, then reached down for her briefcase. Her hands, she noted with annoyance, were trembling slightly, and she felt something hot and tingling race through her body as she rose from the table. She straightened her shoulders defiantly. She had come to the Otawnee Valley to do a job, like countless other jobs she had done in the past eight years; it was that simple. And when she was done, she would leave the Valley and never come back.

And she was damned if Mark Somers's pretty face would stand in her way.

Chapter 2

THE SUMMER AIR felt soft against Sharon's face as she and Mark emerged from the inn. She breathed in deeply, letting it soothe her ruffled humor.

"I want to apologize for my rudeness last night," she said with formal precision to the man walking beside her.

"Ah, last night," Mark repeated. He pointed to a surprisingly old and battered Volkswagen and opened the door for her. "I wasn't exactly a paragon of manners myself."

Sharon glanced at him. His eyes were twinkling like his father's had. "I really had no business being there. Not at that hour, without an ID. You had every right to be annoyed."

"Oh, I wasn't annoyed," he said, pushing the door shut behind her. He walked around to the other side of the car and slid into the driver's seat. "At least not with you. Maybe a little with myself—I'd told the guy on the gate to go home early because his wife is expecting. Then when you turned up, I realized anyone could have wandered in and gotten hurt. It's easy to do around the mill."

He turned toward Sharon, and he was wearing a grin

that almost split his face in two. "Does that earn the sympathy vote?" he asked lightly.

Sharon returned his smile in spite of herself. "Very thoughtful of you," she said. She cleared her throat as he turned the key in the ignition. "In any case, I reported you to Byron Somers. As instructed."

Mark laughed, a low, musical chuckle. It was a sound Sharon recognized somewhere deep inside, and an answering chord sounded within her.

"So you did, Sharon," Mark said softly. "So you did."

He looked at her for a moment longer. His eyes matched the sky behind him, and the sun made his sandy curls glisten like gold. His face was saved from perfection by a nose that had been broken in a game, and by that astonishing smile—wide and, Sharon noticed as for the first time, just a little askew. One side rose higher than the other, and it gave him a little-boy look that was both innocent and impish.

Sharon ran her tongue over her lips. Part of her wanted to blurt out: Remember me? I was the kid from across the river you went out with that Christmas vacation. You *do* remember me—you called me by name.

But part of her wanted that whole memory erased from his mind, as it almost had been from hers. Best leave it buried, she told herself firmly. She fussed for a moment with her briefcase, carefully finding a place for it on the floor of the car.

Mark put the ancient VW in reverse and pulled out of the inn parking lot.

They were halfway down the hill, and below them the Otawnee River threw off silver sparkles in the summer sunlight, when he spoke again.

"So Sharon Dysart returns to the Valley," he said quietly. "My first love."

Sharon had been gazing out the window at the boarded-up storefronts that dotted downtown Somerville, trying to remember what had once occupied them. His words were so unexpected that she almost bumped her head on the window.

"I beg your pardon?" she said, incredulous.

"My first love," Mark repeated, glancing at her briefly as he kept steady hands on the wheel. "Don't tell me you don't remember, Sharon. I know it was fifteen years ago, and you've been quite the mover and shaker since then, but we *did* see each other a couple of times."

Sharon stared at him evenly. His blue eyes were shining with amusement, and the broad, tilted grin was back on his face.

"I remember," she said. "One hardly forgets going out with the richest boy in town. But I'm a little surprised that you remember *me.*"

Mark's grin remained in place, but tiny spots of red appeared at the crest of each cheekbone. "Ah, the old your-family-owns-the-city ploy. I guess that's fair. I remember you because you happened to be born gorgeous, and you remember me because I happened to be born rich."

Sharon felt a warmth in her own cheeks. Then suddenly she laughed. "And gorgeous," she said.

"Huh?" Mark glanced at her again.

"And gorgeous," she repeated. "I remember you because you happened to be born rich *and* gorgeous." She looked directly at him, challenging him to laugh with her, and he did. It was a friendly sound. Sharon sat back against the seat more comfortably, with a sense that some dangerous rapids had just been successfully negotiated.

"Why thank you, Miss Scarlett," he said after a moment. "All compliments gratefully accepted. I took you by surprise last night, though, didn't I? And I have to admit it took me even longer to put together the pieces about you. I knew there was something familiar about you last night, when I turned that flashlight on you. I spent half the night trying to put my finger on it. I figured you'd been telling the truth about working here, and this morning I tried to reach Dad to find out what the story was, and they told me he was having breakfast with a Miss Dysart at the inn. Then everything clicked."

"Byron hadn't told you he'd hired me?"

"Nope. You look different, you know," Mark went on, "with your career-lady clothes and your hair back like that—and even, dare I say it?" He reached a hand over and smoothed the hair over her ear with one finger. "Even a touch of gray in it."

Sharon felt a rush of heat where his hand had touched her, and she shook her head slightly, erasing the impression his finger had left.

"It *has* been fifteen years, Mark. You look different, too."

"So it has. And you've been out in the world, haven't you? Paris, if I'm not mistaken. Quite the international celebrities—at least in the world of steelmaking—you and the little husband. What's happened to Monsieur Lacombe, anyway?"

Sharon pursed her lips into a small frown. "We parted company," she said tersely. "Some time ago."

Mark nodded. "Ah. And you took your own name back. It was that bad, huh?" His expression was thoughtful for a moment, and then his cheerful grin returned. "Did you really figure nobody'd recognize you around here?" he asked.

"I'm not trying to be incognito," she said a little stiffly. "I'm sure there'll be a few people around who still know me. But I've been away from the Valley since the fall after I graduated from high school. I've only been back for a few brief visits, and then the last time for my father's funeral. I can't imagine anyone much will recognize me, or care if they do."

"You underestimate us, Sharon Dysart. Half the guys

you graduated with work at the mill now. They'll know you, fear not. Even if you wouldn't give them the time of day when you were growing up here."

Sharon pressed her lips together tightly and looked back out the window. It was turning into a conversation she didn't want any part of.

"Come on, Sharon." His voice was softly teasing now. "Face it. You *wouldn't* give them the time of day. You were holding out for bigger game, weren't you?"

Sharon's mouth opened, snapped shut, then opened again. Is that what he thought? That she had been after his money?

"You don't need to be ashamed or embarrassed, you know, Sharon. We all have trouble coming to terms with who we are. But you have to do it sometime."

Sharon swung her head around to face him. "That's ridiculous and insulting," she said quietly. "I'm a steel-worker's daughter from Otawnee, and that's one reason I am where I am today. I won't say I didn't want to have a better job than my father had—everyone does—but—"

"Hit a nerve?" Mark interrupted.

Sharon focused carefully on the view out the window. They bounced across the railroad tracks and approached the main gate of the mill.

"I don't need to 'come to terms' with anything, Mark," she said finally. "I'm in the Otawnee Valley to do a job that I've done in dozens of other mills in dozens of other places. To me, it's no different from anyplace else."

Mark nodded soberly. He drove through the gate, throwing a quick salute to the guard sitting inside the little booth, and pulled into a parking space.

Sharon tugged at her lower lip with her teeth. "Besides," she went on, "what would *you* know about—"

She stopped, suddenly aware that what she was about to say was well beyond the bounds of the professional relationship she was determined to have with Mark Somers.

Mark turned the ignition off and shifted in the seat, looking at her. "What would I know about what? About coming to terms with who I am? Why would that be easier for me than for anyone else?"

Sharon clenched her hands in her lap, feeling the nails against her palms. She smiled at him, formally, politely. "This really has nothing to do with the job at hand," she said.

Mark looked at her levelly, his diamond-blue eyes glittering. Sharon felt her hands tremble slightly, and she pushed them more tightly together. "That's true," he answered. "So. Shall we?" He gestured at the mill stretched out beyond them.

Sharon took a deep breath. She picked up her briefcase and settled it on her lap, a tangible symbol of her position here and in the world. Mark confused her. And what was going on inside her confused her as well. There was an excitement that seemed to come from being with him, and it seemed to have both everything and nothing to do with what she had once felt for him—that passionate infatuation of her eighteenth year.

"I think we should get one thing straight right from the beginning, Mark," she said. "You're quite right that I look different. I *am* different. I'm hardly the little girl from across the river anymore. I have two graduate degrees. I've written papers on mill modernization for major journals, and I've addressed major conferences. I'm an expert in my field."

Mark's eyebrows rose slightly, and Sharon was aware of how pompous she must sound. She ran her tongue over her lips and cleared her throat, trying to put a little good humor into what she was saying.

"The point is, I have a three-week contract with SomerSteel, and apparently we'll need to work together for much of that time. I'm a professional; I'll do my job the best I can. Which, if past experience holds true, will be pretty damn good." She gave a fierce little nod, as if to reassure herself. "And then I'll go on to the next job." Suddenly Sharon had no idea where she was going with all these words. It had seemed clear at the start—to let Mark know what their relationship would have to be. But now . . .

Mark was looking at her intently.

"And that will be that," she finished up weakly.

Mark nodded. "And that will be that," he repeated thoughtfully. "Well, that seems straightforward enough. The lady has a job to do." He said this last in a deep voice, like an old-time movie cowboy.

Then suddenly his eyes took on a slate-gray hue behind the blue, as if some curtain had dropped into place. "So I suppose I should make my speech now, too. I gather my father has hired you to do your usual number, which I happen to have read about because I do keep up with your professional journals. Well, this mill doesn't need to be modernized. It works just fine as is. And if you propose that we toss everything and everyone out and bring in the robots, you'd better be prepared to fight every step of the way."

Sharon's eyes narrowed. "What I propose will be for the good of the corporation. And you're free to accept or reject my advice. But I strongly suggest you accept it, if you want to remain competitive." Her voice rose defiantly on the last few words.

He looked at her steadily for a moment longer. The lids of his eyes were half closed, as if he was trying to shield any message they might hold from her, and the creases that slashed across his forehead seemed carved in stone.

Then all at once the hardness disappeared, replaced by the charming, lopsided smile. It happened so abruptly that a tiny wave of suspicion swept through Sharon.

"I'd rather we not fight, Sharon," he said. "For old times' sake. I'd rather we get this job done as pleasantly as possible—if it has to be done at all." He raised his eyebrows in question, as if waiting for an answer.

Sharon stared at him. "If you're implying that I should back out of a contract..."

Mark raised both hands, palms toward her. "Not at all," he said quickly. "Not at all. I'm just promising to try to keep my temper reined in, if you'll do the same."

"I always try to maintain a professional attitude," she answered stiffly. She was already regretting the displays of anger she had let him see.

Mark's smile faded slightly. "Of course," he said. "Well, shall we look around?"

He leaned over the seat and rummaged around in the clutter in the back of the car. Finally he pulled out a hard hat with "Mark" written across the front, then another in a cellophane bag that he handed silently to Sharon. She tore off the wrapper and fitted the hat carefully over her dark hair, then climbed out of the car.

It didn't take long for Sharon to realize that Mark Somers wasn't like the mill managers she was used to. He didn't take her elbow as if she might break, leading her carefully over the catwalks and explaining every detail anxiously, as if to a child. Nor did he show the resentment so many of them did over the mere fact that a woman had invaded their territory.

For Mark, she seemed to be just another hand. He showed an easy camaraderie as soon as they entered his mill. His explanations were clear and thorough, taking for granted both her native intelligence and her wide-ranging knowledge about steel mills. And he was impressively familiar with the mill from top to bottom, with every aspect of the work being done. He was on a first-name basis with every employee they encountered; his relationships with them seemed informal but respectful on both sides.

Sharon watched for traces of arrogance—the arrogance of owner to worker, or even the arrogance that she thought she remembered in his face when he had led the Somerville basketball team to two straight Western Pennsylvania championships. There was none. An uneasy respect for him began to take root in her.

She glanced at him out of the corner of her eye as they moved from one building to another. She knew she felt something else as well, something that had nothing to do with respect. But those feelings, those stirrings and tremblings her body insistently produced when he was near, were simply remnants of that long-ago infatuation, she told herself. They had nothing to do with Mark Somers today—or with Sharon Dysart today. She had no doubt that they could be dismissed as easily as she had finally dismissed her infatuation with Jean-Paul. She stumbled over a piece of scrap steel and frowned.

And Mark was right about the mill, Sharon finally had to acknowledge. For its age and size, it worked well. The blast furnaces burned efficiently, turning out steady, stable quantities of hot metal. The railroad "torpedo" cars that transported molten iron from there to the basic oxygen furnace, where it was converted into steel, and the track over which they ran were well maintained. The rolling mills could turn ingots into slabs and slabs into strips accurately and efficiently. There was already a certain amount of computerization, to match orders with production and to track steel as it moved through the mill. The yards were in better shape than most Sharon had seen. But, she told herself firmly, there was still room for improvement—considerable improvement. Whatever Mark Somers's objections might be.

Mark touched her arm as they approached the giant shed that held the basic oxygen furnace. It was Sharon's favorite place, the heart of the mill, where oxygen is blown through molten iron and scrap to create steel, and where trace elements are added to make that steel a particular kind and quality.

"We're coming on to a heat," Mark shouted above the noise of the furnaces. He pointed to a torpedo car that was also moving toward the building with its cargo from the blast furnace. "There's a load of hot metal coming in now. If we get up those stairs fast, we can make it to the pulpit in time to watch!"

Sharon nodded, stuffing her pad and pencil quickly into the briefcase that now hung from its strap over her shoulder. They hurried inside and up catwalks of steel grating toward the huge, cement-mixer-shaped vessel, three stories high, that hung suspended in the center of the shed. Her heartbeat quickened, and she felt her breath coming in little gasps as they climbed. This part of the process always excited her, but there was something else, some other excitement this time, as well. She was aware of Mark's presence beside her, could almost feel the warmth of his body next to her despite the heat of the July day and of the furnaces.

They came up the last flight of stairs, through a metal door, and out onto the wide concrete ledge—the pulpit—that surrounded the oxygen furnace itself. A flashing red light and a beeping siren warned them that a ladle of hot metal, unloaded from the railroad car, was being guided toward the furnace.

Sharon glanced at Mark Somers. He still had a hand on her arm, but he almost seemed to have forgotten she existed. His eyes were fixed on the giant ladle as it moved slowly across the vastness of the shed, hanging from the roof by four hooks, each bigger than a man. The interior of the shed was dim and shadowy even in daylight. A soft orange glow lit the space above the ladle, and Mark's face seemed almost golden.

They stood well back from the open end of the egg-shaped vessel as cranes guided the ladle forward. Mark squeezed her arm gently to get her attention.

"We move about a hundred tons of metal per load," he shouted. "A hundred tons is an average heat for us. We'll fill ten ingot molds from that."

Sharon nodded. She watched intently as the men lined the ladle up with the opening of the furnace, then instinctively backed up a step as they pulled the nozzle of the ladle down. There was a momentary wait as the metal shifted, and then, at first as if in slow motion and then with gathering speed, the hot metal poured out, showering sparks into the air like a Fourth of July fireworks show.

A thick stream of what looked like liquid gold flowed steadily into the great caldron of the furnace. All around, the air sputtered and fizzed with sparks, and heat rose from the vessel in waves. There was a roaring sound, the sound of a massive waterfall.

After a moment the fireworks stopped and were replaced by clouds of thick, black smoke that seemed to hang briefly above the opening, then billow chaotically into the upper reaches of the shed.

Sharon laughed. Her pulse was racing with excitement. Mark Somers turned and looked at her, a joyful expression on his own face. His eyebrows rose in curiosity.

"You really like this, don't you?" he shouted.

Sharon tossed her head in agreement. "It's . . . it's glorious!" she called back. "I've always thought it was like a fairy tale, with invisible giants and dwarves and . . ." She laughed again. "There's so much raw power. And the colors!"

Mark nodded slowly, his gaze steady on her face. "Well," he said more softly now. "Well. What d'ya know. Under that cool, professional exterior a warm heart doth really beat. Just like it used to."

Sharon let her eyes meet his. The pale blue had turned to silver in the uneven light—silver dully polished and glimmering. His face seemed to glitter, too, with sweat from the heat, and his work shirt had damp patches at the inside of the elbows and under the arms and in a small line down the front. The shirt stretched taut across his shoulders, and Sharon could almost see the smooth muscles beneath it. His cheeks had a tinge of red from the furnace.

She felt a crackle of heat in her own body, as though one of the sparks that still jumped occasionally from the furnace had come too close. Mark Somers blinked and reached a hand toward her, and Sharon knew that he must have felt that abrupt, fiery explosion, too. He was so tall, standing before her, outlined by the orange glow. Her fantasies of giants forging their steel in vast underground caverns seemed to come to life at last.

She hardly noticed when the hand he had reached out settled softly on her shoulder. But she knew instinctively what was going to happen when he took a small step forward. She raised her face toward his.

With one hand Mark tipped the awkward hard hat off her head, letting it dangle from his fingers behind her, and he slid his other hand beneath the jacket of her suit, encircling her waist and pulling her hard against him. Sharon felt the pulse again in her throat. Oh no! The words flashed through her head and disappeared. There was no time to think anything more.

She closed her eyes and opened her mouth to his; she could feel the yielding hardness of his lips as they pressed against hers, the tantalizing taste of his tongue as it began, first tentatively and then urgently, to explore.

Dizzying warmth billowed up within her. She was eighteen and he was barely twenty, and he was everything she had always wanted . . . She reached for him to steady herself. Her hands clutched at his waist, one on either side, and the soft, smooth leather of his belt was reassuring to her touch. Against her thighs, through the linen of her skirt, she could feel the ridges of his corduroy pants, and the hardness of him against her belly. She felt enclosed by heat and dampness and noise, a moist warmth rising in waves from his body and from her own, and the overpowering breathing of giants, the hissing of the oxygen blowing through the steel...

Her whole body trembled as they kissed, and then the hissing stopped. The heat was over in the furnace, and Sharon abruptly blinked her eyes open. She was not eighteen. She was thirty-three, divorced, independent, professional. She pushed Mark away, and almost at the same moment Mark stepped back. It was as if they were controlled by the same forces that made the steel, forces that could bring them to a precise temperature and then somehow recognize that further heat would harm them, would make the delicate metal crack.

Sharon reached unsteadily for the railing behind her. Mark caught her elbow with one hand and held her briefly, just until her legs were once again firm. She stared first at the concrete beneath her feet, then at the man standing facing her.

His smile was awkward, and one hand still clutched her hard hat. "Well," he said almost in a whisper. Sharon barely heard him over the noise of the furnace. "My, my."

Sharon nervously glanced around. To her immense relief, she realized they were standing in shadow, far enough away from the men who were busily tending the furnace not to have been noticed. She looked back at Mark.

"I—I can't think..." she began.

"What? Why you kissed me back?" Mark's smile broadened, and his cheerful poise seemed to reappear.

"Maybe because you wanted to. The same way I wanted to kiss you."

Sharon shook her head fiercely. "It was a terrible lapse from professionalism," she said primly, her voice firmer. She shook her shoulders slightly, letting the tailored lines of her wide-shouldered jacket fall back into place.

Mark's smile turned into the little-boy grin. "Ah, yes, let us not be unprofessional."

Mark held out her hard hat to her, and she snatched it from him, avoiding the touch of his hand as though it might burn. Without another word, they moved across the suspended ledge to its opposite side and watched over the railing as the contents of the furnace were emptied back into one of the massive ladles.

They followed along beneath the ladle as it swung slowly across the shed to the ingot molds, hollow rectangles eight feet deep and some ten inches across, then emptied its molten contents into them. Sharon made a few notes on her pad, but if what she was seeing had not been so very familiar to her, she would not have comprehended any of it. Her mind was racing furiously, trying to understand why she had done what she had done, why this compelling and confusing attraction to Mark Somers seemed still to exist after all these years.

He was, she told herself sharply, just another mill manager in a long line of managers she had worked with. And he was far from being the first who had found her attractive. A few of them had even led her to understand that her contract depended on her going to bed with them—an inference she always responded to with icy disdain. Just because Mark had excited her in this way once before, long ago . . .

Only Jean-Paul, and then only at first, when his charm had been so appealing—only Jean-Paul had made her feel this kind of tingling. But the tingling had died a quick death when she had realized what her new husband was really like. After that, she had never responded to him with this kind of spontaneous wonder again—as he had so frequently pointed out.

"Anything else you want to see before the lunch meeting?" Mark's voice was slightly raised, and Sharon blinked. He must have asked the question at least once before.

"No," she answered uncertainly. "At least..." This is ridiculous, she thought with irritation. She abruptly turned to face Mark. "No. Thank you, there's nothing more. How much time do we have?"

Mark glanced at his watch. "Half an hour."

"Is there someplace I could go over my notes?"

Mark nodded. "My office," he said. "I won't be using it for a while."

He led her out of the big shed and past the open-sided rolling mills, back to the building near the parking lot. Sharon avoided looking at his face, but she could hardly avoid seeing his strong hands as he pushed doors open ahead of her, holding them politely and occasionally dipping his head in a little bow.

His office was large and comfortably messy. He ushered her in, blew some imaginary dust off the old leather swivel chair, and pulled the papers that covered his desk into a pile. Then, with a final nod and a grin, he disappeared out the door.

Sharon studied her notes earnestly. But no matter how hard she tried, she could not shake the image of Mark Somers from her mind: his skewed grin, his glittering eyes, his thick curls. She could feel the touch of his mouth on her own, the warmth of his hand on her arm and back, the way her mouth had yielded to his, the astonishing excitement she felt in his presence.

She realized with an abrupt rush of muddled emotions that something different, something more powerful was at work here than what she had felt for him fifteen years

ago. It was different, too, from what she had felt for
Jean-Paul when they had first met. It was something
inexorable, unstoppable, like the movements of the great
rolling mills once an ingot had begun down their tracks.
It frightened her.

After half an hour a secretary pushed open the door.
Sharon raised her head, and her eyes met a picture hanging on a side wall that she hadn't noticed before. It was
a photo of a couple on a sailboat—Mark, his tangled
hair wet and his long, well-muscled body naked except
for a bright blue bathing suit; and a woman with thick
blond hair, a face Sharon admitted was very pretty, and
a perfect tan. Sharon felt a twinge of curiosity about the
woman—and she felt something else. If she hadn't known
better, she would have said she was jealous.

"Excuse me, Miss Dysart? Your meeting is about to
start."

Sharon blinked, then smiled at the girl in the doorway.
"I'm sorry. Yes, I'm ready." She gathered her notes into
neat piles and tucked them into the proper files in her
briefcase, then stood up. Why hadn't it even occurred
to her that Mark was . . . involved? Maybe even married.
Yes, undoubtedly married. What an idiot, to assume a
handsome, rich, personable man of thirty-five was free.

"Thanks," she murmured.

The meeting was upstairs in an elegant, dark-paneled
room with a buffet table set up at one end and a large
conference table down the middle. Sharon's brain clicked
efficiently as Byron introduced her: the vice-president
for sales; the vice-president for production; the comptroller; the public relations man; the manager of the Number Two facility; and the only other woman in the room,
the personnel officer. A quick glance around told her
that Mark Somers was not here yet.

Sharon took a little of everything from the buffet—
some roast beef and salad, some mixed fruit, and a cup
of coffee—then settled herself in a chair midway down

one side of the big table. She sat quietly as some routine business was dispensed with, sipping her coffee and glancing from face to face, watching the corporation officers talk. Her mind filed each face into its own neat little cubbyhole. She had learned never to take notes at general meetings, where it might call attention to her or inhibit someone from talking freely.

Finally Byron Somers leaned back in his chair and pressed his fingertips together.

"I want to explain Miss Dysart's presence here," he said, smiling jovially around the table. "As some of you may know, she is a consultant on mill modernization. An excellent record—Penn State, MIT, a business degree in Paris, eight years of experience here and in Europe. Highly recommended." Byron looked at Sharon and beamed.

The door to the room opened quietly, and Mark Somers slipped in. He moved quickly to a vacant seat at the end of the table. Sharon followed his movements uneasily, and a stirring at the base of her belly made her shift slightly in her chair. Mark still wore his work clothes. Sweat still glistened on his brow and dampened his shirt, and his sandy halo of curls sparkled with moisture. He seemed to bring some kind of heat with him into this room filled with cool, suit-clad men and women.

He caught Sharon's eye and winked at her. She swung her gaze abruptly back to Byron.

Byron was continuing to talk. "I've signed a contract with Miss Dysart—that is, with Dysart, Incorporated—to do a preliminary evaluation of Number One."

"Sharon—Miss Dysart—grew up right here in the Otawnee Valley," Byron went on, a pleased expression on his face. "In fact, she tells me her father worked right here at SomerSteel Number One!"

Sharon let the air out of her lungs in a long, silent sigh.

"He was a foreman, was he, my dear?" Byron asked.

Sharon shook her head slowly. "No, Mr. Somers. He worked shifts. Just a hand."

"Ah." Byron nodded. The smile on his face was still fatherly—patronizing, Sharon thought—and she bristled a little. Just the way she'd always thought Byron Somers must be.

"Well, my dear, as I told you at breakfast, we're all delighted to have you here again. Sharon's dad used to sneak her in to watch the furnaces!" He looked around the table again, his hands folded in front of him, making sure everyone was as happy about that as he seemed to be.

The others were looking at her now, and Sharon smiled back at them, but the smile was tense. The expressions on their faces were just what she might expect after such a speech: curious, a little doubtful. Before, they would have accepted her as a fellow professional, young as she was. But now . . . A girl whose father was a shift worker here at SomerSteel? Come to tell them what to do with their mill?

Her gaze reached Mark Somers. She couldn't quite identify the expression on his face, but she thought with a touch of wonder that it might actually be sympathy.

The meeting ended moments later. Several of the officers murmured polite welcomes to Sharon as they filed out of the room. She remained in her seat after they had left, shuffling through papers in her briefcase. There was a knot in her stomach as big as a fist.

"You're angry."

Mark's voice cut sharply through the silence in the room. She hadn't even realized he was still there, and she looked up at him in surprise.

"Of course not," she said quickly, one hand still clutching the papers. "Why would I be angry?" The smile on her lips felt pasted there.

"Because my father told them all who you were. Because he called you Sharon and 'my dear' instead of Ms.

Dysart. Because somehow he managed to make you—and all of *them*—think about the employee picnics every summer, when all the kids get balloons and candy, compliments of the boss. Because you've worked all these years to get somewhere—maybe even to get to this exact place, on an equal footing with old Byron Somers—and you find it just doesn't work that way. He put you right back where you started."

Sharon stared at him. He was absolutely right. She had spent fifteen years at it, and Byron Somers had taken ten minutes to make her feel like a kid again—and a kid from the wrong side of the river, at that. Just the way she had felt all those years ago when Byron had told her on the phone that his son wouldn't be seeing her anymore.

"I don't know what you're talking about," she said resolutely.

Mark smiled. "Yes, you do. I've been there myself."

Sharon's eyes widened. She looked at Mark and saw him the way he had looked fifteen years earlier—so sure of himself, so handsome, so loved.

"You!" she blurted. "You couldn't possibly know—" She stopped, as she had stopped herself from saying almost exactly the same thing earlier in the day: How could a rich kid like you know anything at all about how I feel?

He waved a hand in the air. "You don't have a patent on that stuff, you know. Maybe nobody understood you, how ambitious you were, how you wanted to make something of yourself. Maybe you felt as if you had to fight every inch of the way. But even we wealthy folk aren't happy *all* the time."

"I didn't mean . . ." Sharon blinked, and this time she saw Mark's face as it was now, with the creases across his forehead, the shimmer of gray behind his laughing eyes. "I'm sorry."

Mark grinned. "I know you 'didn't mean.' It just gets boring having people assume that money solves all prob-

lems. In any case, try to ignore my father. He has a good
heart. He really thinks he fulfills his social responsibilities with those damned picnics."

Sharon fumbled with the latches on her briefcase and
nodded. She felt a sudden rush of sympathy for Mark,
as she had felt one for his father that morning. There
seemed to be something strong and loving between them,
even though they clearly didn't always understand each
other. And she knew something about love—and mis-
understanding—between fathers and children.

"I kind of liked those picnics," she said softly, looking
up at Mark and smiling.

"I did, too, if you want to know the truth," he agreed.
"Still do."

He had his hands stuck casually in the back pockets
of his corduroy pants, and the fabric pulled tightly across
his thighs. The sleeves of his denim shirt were rolled up
almost to the elbow, revealing smoothly muscled forearms with a faint golden down covering them. The blue
of the faded shirt was a little deeper than the color of his
eyes, and the crown of wild curls gave him the air of
one of those sly, knowing cherubs the Renaissance artists
were so fond of.

Suddenly Sharon laughed. Mark looked at her curiously.

"Something funny?" he asked.

Sharon shook her head. "No, it's nothing." She certainly wasn't going to tell him he looked like an angel,
she thought, amused. She snapped the latch of her briefcase shut, then shook her head again, this time more
briskly. "No. You were right, you know. I *was* angry."

"Of course you were. You had every right to be. It's
just that when, like my father, you've never had to worry
about money, when you've known you were going to
own the family business since you were age five..."
Mark shook his head and looked away for a moment,

then looked back at Sharon and grinned. "Sometimes you're not quite as sensitive as you should be."

Sharon felt the smile tighten on her face. The memory of their ever-so-brief courtship raced through her head again. "And you're different of course, because you were all of *six* when you figured out you'd own the town. Right?"

Mark ducked his head, but not quickly enough to shield something that looked like hurt from Sharon's eyes. "God knows I'm not perfect. I do my best," he said softly. "But anyway . . ." He looked up at her again, and his expression was thoughtful, almost gentle. "Everything's okay now?"

She studied him a moment longer. "Just fine," she said with a little shrug.

He took a step forward, and Sharon raised one hand toward him, almost unconsciously. She wanted to touch him again, wanted to feel the warmth of his skin, the dampness of his shirt; she wanted to run a finger along the creases of his forehead; she wanted to bury her hands in his tangle of curls.

Suddenly she knew that she wanted these things urgently, desperately, more than she had ever wanted anything before. But the urgency and desperation were fighting against the years she had spent learning the hardest of lessons: There is only you. There is no one else you can really trust.

It was a knowledge that had begun fifteen years earlier, when Mark Somers had exploded into her life for two short evenings—and then disappeared.

The door to the room opened, and the secretary stuck her head in.

"Excuse me, Mark. There's a call for you in your office. Important. Oh, and Miss Dysart, Mr. Somers asked me to show you the office you'll be using while you're here."

Mark blinked and pursed his lips, then turned his head to smile at the young woman. "Right, Donna. I'm on my way." He gave Sharon a little bow. "Maybe we'll meet again sometime," he said with a lift of his eyebrows. "Around the mill."

Chapter 3

SHARON'S OFFICE WAS sparsely furnished but acceptable: carpeted, with a big metal desk and swivel chair, a rather worn couch, and an old filing cabinet. The best part, as far as she was concerned, was the window, a large, dusty rectangle facing out over the parking lot, with a direct view of the open side of the hot strip mill. She could stand and watch the red-orange slabs move back and forth on the track to her heart's content.

She smiled wryly at the thought. What a thing for a grown woman to want to do! And she felt a twinge of regret at the thought that the hot strip mill would almost certainly be one of the first things to go if SomerSteel accepted her recommendations, replaced by a continuous casting operation.

Spreading her papers on the desk in front of her, Sharon realized with a stab of annoyance that she had left her portable microcomputer in the trunk of her car— and the car in the parking lot of the Otawnee Inn. She banged one palm on the top of her desk. It was a measure of how much the Somers family discomfited her that it hadn't even occurred to her until now what driving to the mill with Mark might mean. No computer, and, even more annoying, no ride home.

With a small, resigned sigh, she pulled a pad and pencil from her briefcase and began going through a pile of reports and statistics she had requested from the efficient Donna. She worked steadily and carefully, leaving the office only once, halfway through the afternoon, to hunt down a cup of coffee. She pushed aside the questions that kept making their way into her head and refused to let her mind seek answers to them: What had Mark Somers been doing in the years since they had known each other? Had he married, and was the woman in the picture downstairs his wife? She waved a hand in front of her face as if brushing away a persistent fly.

Finally, Sharon stood up, stretched, and looked at her watch. It was after five—and still no ride home. From the window she could see that the hot strip mill was momentarily down; it was the middle of a shift, and there wasn't much activity in the parking lot, either. A single man sat in a chair by the little guard booth reading a book, his long legs stretched out in front of him. She smiled. Even when security was on, it looked none too stringent. But that was no concern of hers.

Her shoes, long since kicked off, had gotten nudged way under the desk. Sharon leaned over and reached for them, then knelt, and finally concluded that they could be more easily retrieved from the other side. She crawled around the desk and, her back to the office door, reached underneath for her shoes.

"My, my," a male voice said cheerfully.

Sharon jerked her head up so quickly she banged it on the underside of the desk. Mark Somers stood in the doorway, leaning against the frame, his arms folded across his chest and a hearty grin on his face.

"Lose something?" he asked sweetly.

Sharon glared at him. "Do you always walk into rooms without knocking?" she asked wearily, rubbing the top of her head. She rocked back on her knees, the errant shoes dangling from one hand.

"Actually the door was open," he said. "A little."

Sharon climbed to her feet. "Was it. Well, you must have had a lovely view." She tucked in her blouse where it had pulled out of her skirt and slipped on her shoes. Mark continued to grin.

"What can I do for you, Mark?"

He looked at her a moment longer, nodding his head. "You have a nice bottom," he said thoughtfully. "You're a good kisser, too."

Sharon's eyes narrowed, and she pressed her lips together in annoyance, but at the same time she felt a twinge of amusement. "Can I do something for you, Mark?" she repeated firmly.

He blinked, as if hearing her for the first time. "Oh, no, actually I thought I'd better do something for *you*. It's time to quit, and you don't have a car down here."

"Yes?" Sharon looked at him quizzically.

"Well, may I offer you a ride to the inn?" He bowed low with a flourish of his hand.

Sharon turned her back and began gathering up the papers on her desk. The memory of their kiss hung in the air before her like a mist. Her hands trembled as she stacked her notes and stuffed them into her briefcase.

Mark watched her. "You don't really need to clear out the office every night," he said patiently, as if explaining things to a slightly dim child. "It can be locked. And anyway, no one is all that interested."

"I have to work on these later," Sharon answered, her back still toward him. "I left my computer in my car."

"Ah. Even so, you don't really intend to work tonight, do you? Your first evening back home?"

Sharon winced and glanced back at Mark. He still stood in the doorway; he hadn't moved into the room at all. His eyes were half closed, and for the first time she noticed how thick his lashes were, and how long. His face was full of color, partly summer tan and partly a healthy glow that ran along his cheekbones and outlined the planes of his face. She looked back at her desk, frowning, and nibbled at her lower lip.

"I even thought we might get dinner somewhere," Mark went on when she didn't answer. "As you no doubt remember, Somerville isn't Paris, gastronomically speaking, but we could probably . . ."

He paused. "Excuse me," he said a little more loudly. "Miss? Do you speak? I could have sworn I heard your voice earlier in the day, but I might have been mistaken. I've just invited you to ride home with me, and for dinner."

"What would your wife say?" The words came out without planning, without thought.

Mark snapped his mouth shut. "My wife?" he said after a brief pause. "Hardly anything, I should think. Since she's not married to me anymore." He looked at Sharon curiously. "What brought *that* up?"

Sharon shrugged, knowing her embarrassment showed. "I don't know why I said that. I'm sorry. I—I didn't even know if you *were* married."

"Well, at least we know she speaks," Mark cheerfully exclaimed over his shoulder to some imaginary presence. "And now that my former wife is dispensed with, how about dinner? I promise to be a good boy, and I *could* provide you with explanations for some of that stuff you've been plowing through today."

Sharon flipped the latches on her briefcase and faced Mark. His expression was amiable and innocent. She knew he could help, and his help could save her time. But it would be playing with fire. She smiled grimly at the image; behind her, beyond the window, the great blast furnace burned.

"Thanks," she said finally. "I do have to eat. And sometimes fraternizing with the enemy is a useful exercise."

The remark was meant to amuse, but Mark lowered his head, and Sharon had the impression that she had scored another inadvertant hit—a hurt she had no intention of inflicting.

She smiled uncertainly. "I mean, after what you said this morning about opposing modernization..." Her voice trailed off in confusion. Then, more firmly, she said, "Maybe you could even explain just why you're so dead set against what I'm here to do."

"Maybe I could," he replied. "And anyway, as you say, we all must eat." He winked at her. His smile had already returned.

As Mark backed the elderly Volkswagen out of its space and launched it toward the front gate, Sharon again noticed the security guard, his chair propped against the side of the booth and a book in his hand. She squinted at him through the windshield. There was something familiar about his gangly legs and the way his glasses rested halfway down his nose.

The man looked up as they came abreast of him, and Mark raised one hand in a salute. "'Night, Al," he called across Sharon.

"Stop!" she cried suddenly. Mark stepped on the brake, and the car jerked to a halt. "Al?" she said tentatively to the guard. "Al Romanelli?"

The man in the chair looked at her, eyes wide behind his glasses, and then a smile split his narrow face, and he was beside the car in two strides.

"Well, Sharon Dysart! Bless my soul. I surely never expected to see you in the Valley again!" He leaned down and grinned at both of them through the car window.

Mark looked back and forth from Sharon to Al. "You know each other?"

"For sure," the man replied. "Used to read poetry together in high school. She edited the yearbook, and I edited the newspaper." He pushed his glasses up his nose with one finger. His smile looked a little shy now. "Guess we were about the only real friends either of us had. Right, Sharon?"

Sharon nodded eagerly, but she felt discouraged, too. "I can't believe it's really you, Al! I thought you'd left the Valley years ago."

"Never did. Went off to Pitt, of course. But when I finished college, there just wasn't any place I'd rather be, when it came right down to it." He shook his head. "But now *you*. I thought we'd seen your tail."

"I have a contract here," Sharon explained hastily. "A three-week contract. I'm a modernization consultant for the steel industry, and SomerSteel..." She spread her hands in a little shrug. "They made me an offer I couldn't refuse," she finished dryly.

The thin man nodded and pushed his glasses up again. "So you stuck with the mills," he said. "You always said you'd figure out some way to do it. Me, too." He waved an arm toward the yards behind them. "Who woulda thought? Anyway, you're a sight for the proverbial sore eyes, let me tell you. Hey, can you come by for supper one of these days? You gotta meet my wife."

"Absolutely," Sharon agreed. "I'd like that."

Al smiled through the window a moment longer. "Modernization, huh? Not planning to replace me with a machine, are you?"

She shook her head sharply. "That question seems to come up with irritating frequency around here," she said, glancing at Mark. "No. Your job is one I've got nothing to say about, Al."

Mark leaned across Sharon, his arm resting on the back of the seat. "How's Jeannie?" he asked. Sharon was acutely conscious of his arm where it barely touched the back of her neck.

Al nodded. "Doin' fine, thanks. And thanks again for last night. It's not like her, but she just wanted me home."

"No problem. Say hi for me." Mark shifted the car into gear and pulled forward with a final wave.

"I'll see you soon!" Sharon called.

Al gave a salute. "Terrific!" He settled back into his chair, book in hand.

"He's a terrific guy," Mark said as they crossed the railroad tracks and left the mill behind. "High school boyfriend, was he?"

Sharon shook her head. A little frown played at the corner of her mouth. "Nothing like that. Just what he said—a friend. We understood each other."

"When no one else did?" Mark's voice was gentle.

"I suppose." She shrugged. "I know I was really lonely my senior year, after he left." And after *you* left as well, she wanted to add.

Sharon was silent. There was a weight inside her, something heavy and discouraging. Mark scooted the little car in and out of downtown Somerville traffic, then pulled into a parking space in one of the municipal garages.

"Why so quiet?" he asked, turning off the motor and shifting in the seat to face her.

Sharon shook her head. "I guess I'm thinking about Al. He really was about the only friend I had when I was growing up. He thought it was okay that I liked the mill, and I thought it was okay that he read poetry. I didn't have to play cheerleader for him."

"Yeah." There was something wistful in Mark's voice, but Sharon hardly heard it. "Must have been nice to have someone who understood you."

"And now, look at him," she went on. "Back exactly where he started. A watchman at a steel mill, with a wife—"

"And two kids and another one on the way," Mark finished for her. "You have a problem with that?" His voice was suddenly sharp, no longer wistful.

Sharon turned to face him. His pale eyes had deepened to sapphire, and the tension in his face caught her off guard.

"He was *smart,*" she said, as if that explained everything.

"So he should have run for the nearest exit, like you did? Is that what you think?"

Sharon looked at Mark curiously. "I suppose it's something like that," she said carefully. "Why does that make you angry?"

Mark turned away for a moment and watched someone climb out of a car across the garage. When he looked back, his expression had softened a little. "Don't throw it *all* out, just because you had some hard times, Sharon. There's a good life to be lived around here. Maybe not all the restaurants and movies you want, but a good life nevertheless. We even let people read books, if they behave."

"That's not the point. The point is—"

"The point is they'll never let him join the country club?" Mark's voice was even, but Sharon could sense the bitterness in it. "Is that the point? Is that so important, Sharon?"

Sharon shook her head fiercely. "Would you mind letting me finish? The point is, he . . ." Suddenly it seemed crazy, trying to explain about ambition and proving oneself and making one's place in the world to someone who had always had a place in the world, who hadn't needed to climb anywhere at all. And besides, maybe it *was* about getting into the country club, if she really let herself think it through.

She shook her head again, this time without much energy. "Never mind. It's not important." With an effort, she turned to him and smiled brightly. "Anyway, I'm starving!"

Mark's light blue eyes remained on her face a moment longer; he seemed to be searching for something more. Then he smiled, too. "Right," he said. "Let's get some dinner."

Sharon had anticipated eating as fashionably and expensively as Somerville could provide. But Mark led her instead to a small, comfortable restaurant on a corner in the middle of downtown, a place she remembered well from her childhood. It has been popular for its ample portions of Italian food. It was not the sort of place she would have expected Mark Somers to frequent—but she was learning every moment that Mark Somers rarely did what she expected him to.

They talked idly about the food over bowls of savory minestrone, platters of homemade linguine with white clam sauce, and white wine.

"My father and I would eat Sunday dinner here," Sharon remembered with a laugh. "It was always wonderful. No matter what we were arguing about that week, we'd always drop it for a couple of hours while we ate."

"Argued a lot, did you?" Mark asked.

Sharon shrugged. "He loved the mill, but he couldn't see any future in it. Especially for a girl." She made a face. "He kept wanting me to take a typing class. Actually," she added, smiling, "he was right. I should have."

They smiled at each other, small, tentative smiles, as if they had just learned something both ordinary and special about each other. Sharon felt the little leap of her heart that she had felt that morning—a spark, almost, that seemed to set her whole body tingling.

"But I don't remember seeing *you* here," she said a little too defiantly, covering her confusion.

"Hah!" The word seemed to explode from him. "Sunday dinners were country club affairs for us. I only got to come here for spaghetti late at night, when no one else was looking. Who saw you do what was very important in my family."

Sharon nodded, feeling for the first time a sense of how Mark's advantages might have made his life more complex. "I remember you were always surrounded by people. Other kids. Until . . . until we went out, you were a very intimidating presence." She smiled, remembering.

"You mean you noticed me before that?" he asked, his little-boy grin suggesting that the idea charmed him. "I hated every minute of it—all those people watching my every move." He leaned forward, his elbows on the table. "That's why you fascinated me so much. For one thing, you were from Otawnee. I figured you hardly knew who I was, and if you did, you didn't care." He leaned back again in his chair. "And then, of course, you were the most beautiful girl I'd ever seen."

"Oh, I knew who you were," Sharon said, ignoring the compliment. "How could I avoid it? You were in the newspaper every other day. You, or your sister, or your mother, or your father. And everyone always talked about you at the basketball games."

Mark shook his head. "Even in Otawnee," he said.

Sharon laughed. "You underestimate the Somers family fame and influence, Mark. Or maybe it was just that you were the best basketball player around."

"Yeah, but it was different with you, no matter what you say." Mark's voice was earnest, and there was a seriousness in his expression that intrigued her. She remembered how that same kind of seriousness—that hint of something more, something deeper—had fascinated her that Christmas of her eighteenth year.

"*You* were different. You had this nervous energy, and you kept yourself kind of, I don't know, separate. The same way you do now." He grinned his tilted grin at her.

Sharon looked down at her plate and sipped her coffee. Then why didn't you fight for me if you felt so strongly? she wanted to ask. Why did you disappear after two dates? *Was* it your father, telling you what to do?

She shook her head sharply. That was all fifteen years in the past. "I heard you didn't come back to the Valley after college. What did you do?"

He shrugged, and his grin widened. Sharon felt another little charge of electricity run through her. "It's really not that interesting," he said. "Your basic youthful rebellion. I went out west, bummed around some. Worked the mills out there and learned the trade. Pretended I didn't have a steel business of my own hanging around somewhere in the background. I didn't want to be rich. Didn't want to boss people around. Didn't want to *be* bossed around."

Sharon narrowed her eyes at him, but he was looking away. Was he saying something about what had happened between them—about his father? She suddenly wished she knew what had happened that Christmas Eve.

"And how about you?" he said abruptly. "How the hell did you end up married to Lacombe?"

Jean-Paul's image flashed into Sharon's head—his classically handsome features, the European clothes that clung so fashionably to his wiry frame. The way he looked directly at you, making you feel like the only person in the world—until he turned to look at someone else exactly the same way. She smiled at Mark.

"He was a guest lecturer at MIT. On international business. He was..." She smiled and bit her lower lip, then blundered on. "He was gorgeous." She remembered that she had used the same word about Mark that very morning.

"Ah," he said. "Another one. So you're just a sucker for gorgeous men."

His chin rested on his hand, and he was watching her talk, his gaze directed on her face, amused and warm and interested. The paleness of his eyes in the dim restaurant light was almost hypnotic.

"I thought he was terrific," she said. She felt somehow compelled to continue. She hadn't talked about Jean-Paul in three years, she marveled. She hadn't even *thought* about him in years. "And after the lecture, I asked him a lot of questions, and—"

"One thing led to another," Mark finished for her, waggling his eyebrows and tapping an imaginary cigar.

"Something like that." Sharon leaned forward in her chair, drawn into the depths of his eyes.

"Didn't you know the guy was a crook?" Mark's tone was unexpectedly sharp and just a little insulting.

Sharon leaned back. "What a thing to say! That's unfair and . . . and . . ." She swallowed and looked away for a moment. His words had broken the spell, and she thought carefully now about what she was saying. "Actually, I didn't know much of anything at all. When I married him I thought I was terribly wise. But I wasn't. Anyway, I had my own interests," she concluded lamely.

"Ah. So you'd found your bigger game."

Sharon felt a hint of warmth suffuse her cheeks. "Maybe so," she murmured. How was it that he could find her weak spots so easily? "At any rate, he was the first man who seemed to find my obsession with steel mills appealing." She smiled ruefully. "And he was ever so charming."

Mark's laugh was short. "Charming. Terrific. Just what you want in your husband, charm. You really weren't quite as smart as you looked, were you?"

Once again, Sharon pulled herself back. It's what you get, she told herself, for letting down the old defenses. No one *really* understands.

She looked at Mark defiantly. "I wasn't much of a judge of charm. Back then I hadn't seen a whole lot of it. Except from you."

Blushes of red appeared high on Mark's cheekbones. "Bull's-eye," he said. "I remember working pretty hard at it with you. Let's see. We went to that concert over in Youngstown. Classy stuff. And then dancing, wasn't it? And Chinese food? I wanted to sweep you off your feet. But your feet were pretty firmly on the ground. Moving ever forward, they were."

Sharon felt a sudden blaze of anger. "Let's be fair, Mark," she said evenly, keeping her voice under control with some effort. "I didn't walk away from you." Wine and anger combined to give her a courage she rarely indulged in personal matters. "In fact," she went on, "I'd be fascinated to hear just what did happen. I only talked with your father, you know. The last I knew we were supposed to go to the country club."

"Ah, yes. The country club raises its ugly head once again." Mark smiled his wonderful, impish, lopsided grin. "But don't tell me the lady's been carrying a torch all these years," he teased. "Waiting for her man to return. If I'd only known..."

Sharon wanted to be angry. She wanted to feel righteous indignation. He had taken her out twice. When she had called, as requested, to tell him what color dress she'd be wearing for their third date, his father had informed her that his son had other plans. She had every right to be angry, she told herself, even though the whole thing had happened years ago.

But she looked at Mark, and her anger faded. His hair was a mess, a tangle of scruffy curls, and his shirt was sweat-stained in several places. He looked about as different from the cool, self-possessed star of fifteen years ago as he possibly could. Maybe he was as different inside as he was outside, she told herself. Or maybe he'd been better inside all along than she'd ever realized.

He stared at her appealingly, tracing the lines of her face, the shaggy thickness of her black eyebrows, the high forehead, the full lips.

"I'm sorry," he said finally. "That was stupid. Forgive me."

Sharon shrugged and nodded. Mark was quiet, taking the last sip of his coffee and patting his mouth with the

napkin, and Sharon was abruptly conscious of his mouth—
the same mouth that had pressed itself against hers a few
hours earlier, that had felt so warm and strong. She
remembered the excited way he had looked at her, recognizing that she shared his delight in the workings of
the great furnaces. A shiver of excitement ran through
her, and the soft down on the backs of her arms seemed
to stand up straight.

Whoa! she told herself. You've been through this
before, and you know where it leads. Maybe you're *still*
not good enough for him—not when it counts. When
push comes to shove, he'll do what his father did at
lunch; he'll let you know you're not really quite his kind.

"Actually, if you want to know the truth, my cousin
arrived in town, and my family insisted I take her to the
dance I'd promised you."

Sharon raised her eyebrows, and Mark held up one
hand, as if in defense.

"I know, it wasn't fair to you, and I'm sorry. I was
due back at college the next day, and...Well, to tell
the truth, maybe I was using you just a little. You maybe
liked me a little better because I was a way out of Otawnee for you. And I maybe liked you a little better because
you were the final weapon in a long, silent war with my
family. When my father insisted I not see you again, I
took off for school and didn't come back. Not for almost
eight years."

Sharon's eyes widened. "'Yes?" she said softly. It
had been the way she'd so often worked it out in her
head. "Just because of me?"

Mark smiled. "I'd like to say yes. But it wasn't just
you, no. It was being my father's son. It was all those
newspaper articles. And all the kids who wanted to be
my friend because my name was Somers. And not being
able to come here for Sunday dinner." He looked at
Sharon and shook his head, chuckling. "I guess it doesn't

sound very tough to you. But I hated being the rich kid in town. I wanted to be one of the real people. Like you."

Sharon nodded thoughtfully. Maybe, just maybe it was all true.

"In a way, we're two sides of the same coin, I guess," he went on. "You wanted to be me, and I wanted to be you. All I ever really wanted was to work down at the mill as a hand, to be accepted by the guys from Otawnee. Don't laugh."

Sharon shook her head. "No. But you came back," Sharon said. "You're still rich, and you *are* the boss, and—"

"Right." Mark tipped his chair back, holding the edge of the table with his hands. "Which gives me access to all kinds of information you need. Want to talk about SomerSteel?"

Sharon had the abrupt impression that Mark Somers had said much more than he had meant to—that these were things he rarely, if ever, talked about. She opened her mouth once, intending to ask him the question she had begun: What were the compromises? What did you give up to come back? But she stopped.

"That would really help me out," she said finally.

It was almost an hour later when they rose to leave. Sharon was exhausted; the drive out from New York yesterday and another long day today—not to mention the wine—had taken their toll. Mark had done what he could to be helpful, answering her questions in straight-forward language, filling in blanks in the reports she had read, and steering carefully away from talking about his own opposition to her work.

"I appreciate all this," Sharon said with a smile, pushing her chair back from the table.

"Anytime." He ducked his head in the little mock bow that was already familiar to her. "Nothing's too good for the lady from Otawnee. And Paris."

They rode silently up the hill toward the inn. Just as they reached the entrance, Mark swung his little car onto the shoulder of the road.

"Want to see my favorite view of the mill?" he asked, eyes wide.

Sharon groaned. "I didn't think there were any new lines in the world. I can't believe you said that."

"No, really!" He nodded earnestly. "There really is a terrific view. It would only take a minute. Right over there, there's a clear path all the way down the hill. Come on, Sharon!" His voice was cajoling, like that of a little boy wanting to show off his favorite toy.

Sharon laughed. "Okay," she said. "But I'm really tired. It can only take a minute."

He pulled the VW to the left, onto a narrow road leading away from the inn, and then left again onto a dirt pathway. They drove for a minute between two lines of trees; then abruptly the trees ended, and the car rolled to a stop at the very crest of the Somerville hill.

Sharon breathed in sharply.

The city of Somerville sprawled down the hill on either side of them: residential neighborhoods up here, the big brick and frame houses of the lawyers and doctors hidden by trees and darkness now; and the center of town below, straddling the railroad tracks next to the river.

The river itself, cleaner than it had been when Sharon was a child, glimmered softly in the moonlight and wound like a snake through the valley. Across the river, climbing the opposite hill, was Otawnee. Its narrow frame houses were jammed together shoulder to shoulder, as if gathering strength from one another against the night. Sharon felt a twinge of sadness as she gazed at the shadowy outlines. Maybe if she hadn't concentrated so much on getting out, she might have had more time to find what was good about it.

She let her gaze fall to the foot of the hill, to the river and the mill yards that hovered on either side of it. The same sounds were in the air that had been there the night before: the heavy, muffled breathing of the blast furnace; the occasional echoing clash of metal on metal; the soft hissing of the rolling mills.

"You know, I like the sounds best of all." Sharon was hardly aware she was speaking.

Mark nodded. "Yeah. I remember lying awake when I was a kid in the summer, listening to the mill."

They were quiet for a moment, hearing sounds they had lived with for so long. A puff of orange smoke rose far below them as a glowing ingot was loaded into the blooming mill.

"You were right," Sharon said softly. "This is a wonderful view."

Far away, at the bottom of the hill, she saw the line of orange begin moving back and forth in the night darkness, disappearing now and again behind the walls of the shed. She had almost forgotten Mark Somers existed until he covered her hand with his own large, strong one, folding hers within it, not letting her go. Sharon swung her head toward him and tried to smile.

"I'm a little tired..." she began, but Mark touched her lips with his other hand, silencing her, and then patted her knee in a gesture that was as tentative and awkward as that of a teenager on a first date.

"Sharon," he whispered, "you're lovely." He kissed her forehead lightly. "How could I have ever let you go?"

Sharon felt the warmth of his lips where they touched her, barely brushing the flesh. He kissed her eyebrows and then, both hands on her shoulders, held her facing him for a moment. He was grinning.

"Anyone with eyebrows like that can't be *all* professional," he said cheerfully.

Mark's hands tightened on her shoulders. His head was tilted slightly to one side, and his eyes, silvery in the reflected moonlight, watched her face with an interest, a sympathy, that seemed to Sharon absolutely genuine.

Her brain sent out a frantic "Watch out!" message, but it barely had time to register before Mark leaned forward and kissed her.

There was steel inside her, something hard-edged and sharp and heavy; she had felt it there all her life. It had kept her moving forward, over and past the obstacles; it had made her cool and strong. But now, as Mark Somers pulled her against him, Sharon felt the steel begin to warm and melt, like pieces of scrap do when they're tossed back into the furnace. The warmth spilled through her body, filling every muscle and limb and nerve with heat and energy, forcing the exhaustion out of her.

Her arms went around him instinctively, her hands pressing against the wide, hard muscles of his back through his denim shirt. She felt his cordlike muscles move beneath her palms as he shifted, turning more squarely toward her in the seat. His mouth felt hot and hard against her own, searching, exploring, waiting for her response, and then searching again. There was a wonderful taste to him—a sweetness that was vaguely smoky; and a smell that suggested hard work and steel mills and pure, old-fashioned soap.

Mark moved one hand on her shoulder until it encircled her throat, the thumb resting gently at the tiny triangle where a pulse thrashed wildly. The other hand he slid down her arm, over the soft cotton of her blouse; then he lifted it again and brought it to rest at the V of her blouse, where her breasts swelled against the fabric.

The touch of his hand there, at the rise of her breasts, brought with it an excitement full of heat and fire, of fireworks and orange flames in the night. She started to pull away from him in fear and confusion, but his hand at her neck held her close, and after the smallest show of resistance she came back to him, yielding her mouth to him and seizing his for her own.

She needed him urgently. She was amazed and over-whelmed, but there was nothing she could do to stop herself. The fire kept coming, burning hotter and hotter, the flames stretching outward from the very center of her being. She pressed her lips to his, opening them for his tongue, letting his teeth nip at her mouth and her tongue; and she returned his touches, using her own tongue to explore his mouth. Her hands held him to her.

Mark's breath came quickly now. Sharon could hear a hoarseness in it as he moved his mouth away from hers and let it drift softly over her cheek, then down her throat to the open collar of her blouse. His moist, warm lips rested there at the small triangle, and she felt a surge of heat race through her body from that spot to somewhere deep inside, somewhere at the base of her belly. She shuddered.

His tangle of curls rested against her cheek as he bent his head, and she buried one hand in it, feeling the grit-tiness of a summer day spent in the mill in its damp texture.

He turned her body toward him against the seat of the old Volkswagen, and Sharon's knee hit the gearshift. The pain was momentary, but it was enough. She pulled away with a sharp intake of breath.

"I'm—I'm sorry," she gasped. "I . . . this is just no good." Her wide eyes focused on Mark's face, and for just a moment she thought she saw there a trace of ar-rogance, of sullenness, remembered from his youth.

He looked at her curiously. "Why not?" he asked. "Just finishing up some old business."

Sharon winced at the callous sound of the words, then shook her head. "There isn't any old business between us, Mark. Only new business. And that's exactly what it's going to stay: business."

She looked away, out the front windshield, but the ingot in the blooming mill had cooled to an invisible slab of gray steel. She glanced back at Mark. Whatever she thought she had seen had disappeared now, replaced by the familiar little-boy grin.

"So when was the last time you played around in a car?" he asked with a chuckle. "For you, maybe never! You surely wouldn't let me get away with anything fifteen years ago. In college? Not, I presume, with the elegant Jean-Paul Lacombe."

His grin was infectious. "No, not with Jean-Paul," she agreed, smiling. There hadn't been much playing around at all with Jean-Paul, not after those first few wonderful months. Not once she had realized what he was all about.

And what he was all about was charm. He had fished for people, made them come to him, and then used them to his own advantage. He wanted to be loved, but his own professions of love were insincere. He had played on his good looks and on his ability to be amusing— two things, Sharon realized, Mark Somers had in spades.

"What did you mean earlier when you asked me if I'd known Jean-Paul was a crook?" she asked suddenly.

Mark shrugged mischievously. "You were married to him. You must have known his reputation, a smart lady like you. Mostly I just wanted to see if I could get a rise out of you. Worked, too."

"Yes." Sharon smoothed her skirt against her knees, then, with a little sigh, went on. "Yes, I did know. Not at first. It took me about six months to figure out that all was not quite as it seemed."

"Meaning?"

"Meaning that Jean-Paul was up to his ears in debt, and that his lovely continental elegance was mostly bought with what is politely known as creative accounting. Meaning that after the French government nationalized most of the Lacombe family mills, he used the money to diversify into all kinds of things." Sharon shrugged. She could hear the hardness creeping into her voice despite her efforts to keep it out.

"So what did you do?"

She folded her hands stiffly in her lap. "I made what was left of the family holdings profitable, paid off the debts. Sliced off what was legitimate from what was . . . not quite. The family was very grateful. They gave me some shares in what was left of Lacombe Industries. Jean-Paul, on the other hand"—she smiled a small, bitter smile—"didn't give me much of anything," she concluded. "I divorced him."

"Whoo." Mark's eyes were wide.

"What does *that* mean?"

"You sound pretty tough."

Sharon shrugged again. The tiredness was returning, moving in waves like the heat had through her body, spreading outward from her neck, her shoulders.

"That's what Jean-Paul used to say. A tough lady." She smiled, but there was no humor in it, and her voice was almost a whisper. "I guess he was right."

Mark patted her knee again. "No," he said tenderly. "No, he wasn't. I'll take you back to the inn."

Chapter 4

THE ALARM JANGLED at seven the next morning, but Sharon pushed the button in and burrowed her head back into the pillow. She had ordered breakfast brought to her room when she had come in the night before, so there was a little extra time available—time to luxuriate in the softness of the bed and in her memories of the night before.

She had slept soundly, without dreams, and she still felt a warmth inside her from the evening spent with Mark, a kind of tingling that occupied her whole body. His face, with its cheerful grin and twinkling eyes, seemed to hover in front of her closed eyes. It made her smile. Whatever he was up to, his presence and his attentions made her feel good.

"Good," she repeated wryly. *Wonderful* was more like it. Just the way he had made her feel all those many years ago.

It was flattering to know he was still attracted to her; it was disconcerting to know she was still attracted to him. Or attracted to him again—maybe that was a more honest way of putting it. Because this time it was a different kind of attraction, more adult, less romanticized. This time she knew what she was about. And this time, she told herself, she was old enough to take it slow. She was old enough to know if it was real or not.

She felt a little giggle in her throat as she remembered the all too real heat she had felt inside herself the evening before.

A knock signaled the arrival of breakfast. She slid her long legs out from under the covers, then sat up in one quick motion and pushed the heavy coverlet aside. The air conditioner had made the room cold during the night, and she picked up her robe from the end of the bed and wrapped it around her shoulders, then gave herself a quick, impulsive hug.

It had been all right, coming back here. Even with the unexpected presence of Mark Somers. Or maybe, she told herself with a cautious smile, because of it.

Sharon took the tray gratefully from the man at the door. She was ravenous, despite the huge meal she and Mark had eaten the night before, and the wonderful breakfast smells of eggs and bacon, muffins and coffee only reinforced her hunger. She set the tray down on the desk, lifted the silver cover, poured out a steaming cup of coffee, and settled down to eat.

The Pittsburgh morning newspaper was tucked at the back of the tray. She scanned its headlines as she buttered her muffin, and as she turned it over, she realized that a second newspaper was folded beneath it: the Somerville *Clarion*. She smiled at the familiar logo. She had read this newspaper every morning of her high school days.

But this time there was no picture of Mark Somers. There was, instead, a picture of Sharon Dysart. Her high school graduation picture. Sharon's hands stopped buttering in mid-muffin, and her mouth dropped open in astonishment. Her gaze flickered to the accompanying article. MODERNIZATION STUDY AT SOMERSTEEL, the headline read; *Former Local Resident to Draw Up Plan*.

She put the knife and muffin carefully down on the plate in front of her.

It was a disaster, plain and simple. Everyone at the mill would be running scared as soon as they saw the article; everyone would assume that all jobs were in danger. Sharon knew all this from experience. It was one reason Dysart, Inc. always insisted on a no-publicity clause in its contracts. As soon as this stuff got circulated, there would be no hope of getting unbiased information.

Sharon unfolded the paper with quick, angry motions. Byron Somers would hear about this. Immediately. She stood and started to reach for the phone, then abruptly stopped, her hand poised in mid-air. Slowly, she sat back down.

Mark. The thought took slow root in her mind. There would be no reason for Byron to do this, but Mark . . . Mark Somers was the only person in town who might have put all this information together in such a short time. He was also the only person in town who knew why she was here and already *opposed* it. Mark, who was certainly clever enough to realize that this kind of publicity would hurt rather than help. Tender, gentle, *charming* Mark.

With a self-discipline nurtured through so many years that it was now instinct, Sharon straightened her shoulders and ate the rest of her breakfast with slow, deliberate bites. She read through the article carefully, occasionally making a note to herself.

When she had finished, she folded her napkin, rose, and walked slowly around the room, gathering what she needed for the day. Then she quickly showered, dressed in gray slacks and a white blouse, and arranged her hair.

She stopped for a moment in front of the mirror, noting with a certain satisfaction the lean elegance of her face with its high cheekbones and deep-set eyes and the sleekness of her pulled-back hair. It was a very different face from the one in the newspaper.

She tucked her wallet into her briefcase, then scooped up the *Clarion* from where it lay on the table and put it carefully into the case's outside pocket.

At the mill, she headed directly for Mark Somers's office. Donna looked up curiously at her approach, and her eyes widened slightly when she caught sight of Sharon's grim face. She started to her feet.

"Can I help you, Miss Dysart?"

Sharon paused for a moment at Donna's desk, her best business smile now in place. "I need to see Mark," she said evenly. "About some questions I need to have answered." Donna made no move to interfere as Sharon pushed the door to the inner office open with a firm hand.

Mark was standing behind his desk, talking on the phone. The light from the window behind him threw gold glitter into his thick hair. Sharon felt the pulse in her wrists begin to speed, and she clenched her hands in anger at the way her body insisted on betraying her.

Mark grinned and winked as she entered.

"Just be a minute," he whispered, one hand shielding the phone receiver. He gestured toward a chair on the other side of the desk.

Sharon remained standing. As he spoke, she pulled the newspaper out of her briefcase and spread it carefully out on Mark's desk.

She glanced at his face, hoping to catch a spontaneous response of some kind, but she caught her own breath instead. She had been quite sure she hadn't dreamed during the night, but now, looking at his face, she knew that she had. Those shimmering blue eyes, the nose with its singular bump halfway down, the slightly off-center grin: all were imprinted on her mind with a clarity that had to have come from hours of dreams. Slightly off-balance, she looked back at the newspaper again.

Mark's eyes skimmed over the article as he continued to talk to his invisible listener. A smile began to play at the corners of his mouth. Finally he hung up the phone with a crisp good-bye.

"Ah, yes," he said, leaning over to study the article more closely. "Our local celebrity. Now *you* know what it feels like to get written up in the paper." Then he did an exaggerated double take as the picture caught his eye. "Whew! Not much of a likeness, though. I think high school pictures really should be against the law. Though, of course," he added thoughtfully, stroking his chin, "that was the face I fell in love with the first time. Hard to believe."

"How did it get there?" Sharon asked. She was working hard to ignore his words and to keep her voice calm.

Mark shrugged and shook his head. "Beats me. Somebody recognized you and phoned a friend, I suppose." He rubbed his hands together and smiled, his eyes still focused on the photo in the paper. "Sure is a gem. So what can I do for you this morning, Sharon?"

"What you can do for me is stop trying to sabotage my work by putting premature publicity in the paper."

Mark looked up, straight at her, for the first time since they had begun to talk. His eyes registered sudden surprise as he saw the stiffness of her expression. "Oh, dear," he said. "And here I thought we were having a friendly little conversation."

His grin slowly faded as Sharon remained silent.

"Hey," he said, *"I* didn't do it. You can't think..." He stopped and looked at the paper again, smiling. "For one thing, I never would have used *that* picture. Besides..."

His grin was back full-blown as he looked up at her, and she felt the sudden tingling in her fingertips that she had felt when she had first seen him, two nights earlier, unrecognized in the parking lot. "What the hell harm does it do?" he went on.

He started around the desk toward her. Sharon folded

her arms stiffly across her chest, and he stopped.

"So people know why you're here. Does it matter, Sharon? They're gonna find out sooner or later anyway. They'll probably be proud of you!"

His unflappable good humor made the anger surge more powerfully through Sharon.

"It matters," she said. "I have a no-publicity clause in the contract precisely because unplanned publicity can get everyone upset, even hostile, and that makes my job almost impossible. I need to be able to circulate freely in the mill. I need to have the employees feel free to talk to me. I need—"

"Oh, come on, Sharon," Mark interrupted. "Don't give me all that. This article won't make a damn bit of difference in how well your job gets done. What *you're* upset about is all this other stuff." He reached over to the desk and picked up the paper.

"Miss Dysart," he read aloud, "is an Otawnee native and a graduate of Otawnee High School, where she was active as a cheerleader and editor of the yearbook. Her father, Howard Dysart, was employed by SomerSteel from 1952 until his death twelve years ago. Miss Dysart left the Valley to attend Penn State University . . ." Mark stopped reading and glanced up.

Sharon could feel the red rising in her cheeks. "That's not true," she said in a voice louder than she intended it to be.

Mark's eyebrows rose. "What's not true? The cheerleader part? The yearbook?" He glanced back at the article. "Your father?"

Sharon shook her head fiercely. "You know that's not what I mean." Her voice was under control, but her cheeks were still warm. What was it about this man that confused her so? "I mean, that's not why I'm angry."

"Oh?" Mark's voice was curious, and there was an absolutely innocent look on his face that, under other circumstances, would have made Sharon laugh. At the moment, it only served to increase her annoyance. "I don't know why not. If somebody put *my* high school picture in the paper, I'd *kill*."

Sharon felt a sudden singleness of purpose that gave her renewed strength. She wanted to make him stop smiling. She wanted that little lift at the corners of his mouth to disappear, once and for all. She reached over and pulled the paper out of his hands, and he jerked back slightly.

"This article will make everyone angry, Mark," she said in a firm, even voice. "Who knows what they might do? They're very physical people."

Mark took a step backward, so he was leaning against the edge of his desk. He folded his arms in front of him. "And just what is that supposed to mean?" he asked quietly.

Sharon shrugged. "It means exactly what I said. They're angry and probably scared and . . . unpredictable."

"If you're implying that anyone around here might take a punch at you, my love, you're dead wrong. Except maybe me, if you keep this up much longer."

"It's happened before," Sharon responded.

"These are my people, Sharon. I know them. It won't happen here."

Sharon opened her eyes wide. "They're not your people, Mark, any more than they're my people. I left them behind, and you were never part of them. You were born rich, and that makes you different."

Mark stared at her, and Sharon stared steadily back for a moment, then finally lowered her gaze to the paper in her hand. "In any case," she went on lamely, "it's against the terms of our contract to put this kind of publicity out."

He continued to look at her for another long moment. Then finally he said, "I didn't do it, Sharon. I don't know who did. I don't break contracts. And whatever battles I have to fight with you professionally I'll fight head on, not through some newspaper article."

Sharon raised her eyes to meet his with a defiant lift of her chin. There was a grayness, almost a cloudiness, about his eyes; the glittery blue had disappeared. So had the little lift at the corners of his mouth. But she felt no sense of having won. She felt about as depressed as she ever had.

"As long as that's understood," she said. With a quick nod, she turned and left the room, and Donna watched her with curious eyes as she moved rapidly past her desk into the hall.

Back in her own office, settled behind the big metal desk covered with scratches, Sharon took a deep breath, then another. She folded her hands firmly in front of her, waiting until they were perfectly still and her heart was no longer beating against the wall of her chest. She knew her cheeks must be flushed; she could feel their warmth.

It was, she told herself wryly, simply remarkable that Mark Somers could still do this to her after all these years: excite her, anger her, make her feel that she wanted him more than anything she had ever wanted in her entire life. It was clear now that last night she had been very close to falling into the same trap she had fallen into fifteen years before. He had said it last night: He had used her then. And he was using her now, using her vulnerability to discredit her work.

She wasn't even entirely convinced that he *hadn't* put the article in the newspaper. She stared at her hands for a moment longer, then straightened her shoulders and sat erect in the old swivel chair. The point was, she told herself firmly, it didn't matter who put the article in the newspaper. It was there, and she had to figure out what to do about it. "And," she said aloud, "I have to forget about Mr. Mark Somers."

Sharon began jotting down a revised schedule in her notebook. The less time everyone had to digest the article and think about what it meant, she knew, the easier it would be to get information. The best thing to do would be to start interviewing employees now, this morning, before they'd had a chance to discuss the article. After a few minutes' work, she picked up the hard hat from the couch where she'd left it the night before and headed out into the mill.

She started at the control booth over the thirty-six-inch strip mill. The two men who sat in the dark, dingy little room had their eyes focused on the television screens in front of them, keeping track of exactly where the slab, thirty feet below them, was going. Their hands rested on the levers that made the slab change direction or added more pressure from the rollers. Neither man turned as she entered.

She pulled up the only extra seat, a straight-back wooden chair with one rung missing, to a spot just behind and between the two men. They nodded a hello to her, eyes still on screens. After a moment, one of the men leaned back in his chair, tapping the other's elbow to indicate he should take over.

"So. You're the bigshot," he said. His expression was curious but not, as far as Sharon could tell in the dim light, belligerent.

Sharon smiled. "I'm Sharon Dysart" she said. "I'm putting together a few figures about the mill. Nothing major. Could I ask you guys a couple of questions?"

The second man glanced over his shoulder at Sharon. "You gonna figure our jobs right out of existence?" he asked.

Sharon drew in a deep breath. "That's not why I'm here," she responded. "I . . ."

The first man shook his head and smiled back at her. "No problem," he said. "Ask away. If anybody's got it safe these days, we do. Anyway..." The man turned his chair to face hers. "Anyone who looks like you can ask me anything she wants. Any little thing at all." He smiled broadly. "Not much resemblance to that picture in the paper this morning."

Sharon wanted to ask why he felt his job was so secure, but her brain warned her to stay away from the issue as long as the men were willing to.

"Do you look like your high school graduation picture?" she asked with a smile.

He shook his head mournfully. "In my case, the world would be a lot better off if I did."

Sharon laughed sympathetically, then pulled out her clipboard. "Do you always work the same shift and job?" she began.

The morning passed quickly and, to her surprise, rather pleasantly. She liked being out in the mill rather than hunched over her calculator and her computer, and she reluctantly had to admit that Mark seemed to be right: There was very little open hostility or fear being shown her. She had often encountered a kind of sullen refusal to cooperate in other mills. Here there was a camaraderie that was, to her professionally critical eye, quite impressive.

But what most impressed her was the sense of security that seemed to exist. Modernization was something to fear, but their own jobs, the workers kept implying, would be secure. Mark Somers would see to that.

The tension Sharon had felt when she first saw the headline in the *Clarion* and that had increased during the confrontation with Mark began to dissipate as the morning wore on. There was something about these people that made her feel almost comfortable, comfortable in a way she hadn't really felt in a long time.

She found herself joking with old high school acquaintances, and they laughed with her over the photo in the newspaper. Others of the men remembered her father, and two of them remembered seeing her as a child right here at the mill, watching wide-eyed as her father led her up to the pulpit to see the fireworks of a heat at the basic oxygen furnace.

Everyone she talked with seemed basically happy with the way the mill was run. And Mark Somers was clearly that rarest of creatures, a well-loved boss.

By lunchtime, Sharon's annoyance with Mark was colored by an overlay of curiosity about him. It was confusing, trying to figure out Mark Somers, even after the years of experience she had had with men who, her rational mind told her, were very much like him.

She sat at a table in the lunchroom, surrounded by men from the strip mill where she had finished up her morning's work, and memories chased their way through her head as she nibbled at her food. She could still feel the touch of his arms against her, of his hand on her breast and his lips against her own mouth.

She shook her head sharply. The men around her were looking at her expectantly.

"Did I miss something?" she asked with a smile.

"Just the usual," a voice called from the end of the table. Sharon glanced at the good-looking young man sitting there. Twenty-two or twenty-three, she guessed. A prime target for layoffs, if they came. She frowned slightly at the thought.

"Somebody wanted to know why you're not married," the young man went on. "Gorgeous broad like yourself."

It was the first time she could ever remember feeling amused rather than annoyed at that question.

"Oh, I tried it," she said with a nod. "I didn't much like it. Maybe I picked the wrong one first time around."

There were sage nods on all sides. "Happens to the best of us," one of the older men agreed.

Several men laughed. "And the worst," one called out.

"Want to try again?" the young man—boy, almost, Sharon told herself—shouted over the general amusement.

Sharon leaned forward and looked down the table at him. She smiled warmly. "Thanks for the offer," she said with a little wave.

A few minutes later she stopped at the trash bin by the door and pushed the remnants of her lunch off her tray. The boy's face stayed with her. It was full of good humor, optimistic, just starting out. Her brow puckered into a frown. It wasn't that she hadn't seen the same face in every mill she had ever worked in; it was just that here, at SomerSteel, it was somehow more real.

A hand touched her elbow. Sharon stepped quickly to one side, getting out of the way, but the hand didn't move. She looked up. Mark Somers stood in front of her.

"Find your culprit yet?" he asked.

Sharon blinked. "My culprit?" she repeated.

"The great anonymous source for the newspaper article," Mark explained patiently. "You remember. The newspaper article that was going to mean your imminent death?"

Sharon looked up at him. He was dressed in a tan corduroy jacket and slacks, and a dark red tie was pulled loose below his unbuttoned collar. This morning, in his office, she had been too angry to notice what he was wearing. He looked, she found herself thinking, even better than he did in work clothes.

"Oh," she said flatly, holding her voice in control. "No. I haven't actually been trying. I've reorganized my schedule to accommodate any possible difficulties."

Mark nodded. "Ah. Any possible difficulties. I see." His face was blank of all expression, neutral. "Well, you're no longer worried, then, apparently."

She swallowed hard, suddenly remembering what she'd said to him in his office—that his wealth kept him from understanding these people. Her morning had begun to prove that he understood them very well indeed.

"I'm still concerned," she said primly.

He nodded slowly. "Are you now. Okay. As long as you're satisfied that I'm not the one to blame." He looked at her evenly for a moment, then let a smile settle on his lips. "In any case, I hear you've been doing some spying on me."

"I don't think I know what you mean," she said.

Mark's smile broadened. "Asking everybody and his brother what they think of the boss," he answered.

"Oh." Sharon waved a hand as if in dismissal. "That's just routine," she said lamely. "It's part of the process. A response-to-management question."

It occurred to her that it had taken Mark just two hours to get feedback on exactly what she was doing. She had never been in a mill where news got reported to the manager so quickly. But then, she was beginning to think that she had never met a manager quite like Mark Somers.

Those are dangerous waters, she reminded herself. Don't forget that Mark is, professionally at the very least, the enemy.

Mark continued to smile at her. "Routine." He nodded. "Well, I hope they're all telling you what I told them to. Otherwise, they know they get beaten up after hours tonight."

Sharon nodded weakly. All she could see was the broadness of his chest in his button-down shirt and the triangle of tan flesh above the open collar.

"I'm sure they will," she murmured. The pulse at the base of her throat was working hard. It was as though his simple presence threw her into a state of bewilderment; her body and her senses seemed all out of control.

She sent a sharp message to her brain to shape up, but the only result was a little flicker of flame somewhere deep inside her belly.

Enough of this, she told herself firmly. She tossed her head back, pushing hair pins more securely into her chignon with one hand, and smiled at him.

"Of course it wasn't quite *all* routine," she said. "I do need to gather my own ammunition, after all." She gave a farewell nod and turned away. But as she moved on down the corridor, she had the sinking feeling that she had somehow drawn lines again for a battle Mark Somers was willing to negotiate off the field.

It was almost four o'clock before Sharon felt like venturing out of her office and back to the mill. She had spent the afternoon looking at her interview notes, trying to collate the few she had on the computer into something resembling a worker-attitude profile. But it was hot, and all she had been able to see in front of her was that little triangle of tan skin at the base of Mark's throat; the strong, square wrists that emerged from the cuffs of his shirt . . .

He had seemed so gentle the night before, and so sincere. But, Sharon reminded herself, he had seemed gentle and sincere years ago, too. He had seemed wonderfully sincere—for two evenings. And then he had disappeared from her life as surely as if he had died. And whether or not it was true that his father had insisted on it, he had agreed.

Finally, Sharon took her hands off the computer keyboard and rubbed her eyes gently with the tips of her fingers. Turning in her chair, she could see the open side of the thirty-six-inch mill shed. A slab was on the track, glowing orange, adding its steamy presence to the mid-afternoon heat.

Suddenly all she wanted in the world was to feel that

heat. She wanted to be at the mill, out of her office, where the July temperatures were making the thirty-year-old air-conditioning system almost inefficient. At least the heat at the hot strip mill would be pure, in its way. And a cup of coffee would be nice. She felt around with her feet for her shoes—kicked off as usual—found them and slid them on.

Steam rose from the track as she entered the shed. It almost obscured the men who lingered along its edges, and the control booth seemed to hang in the air halfway down the track. Through its darkened windows she could see the vague outlines of the men she had spoken to in the morning.

The noise was vast: steam hissing, the rollers creaking endlessly, the slab itself clanging against the edges of the track and hitting the ends with huge metallic thunks.

Sharon barely heard the voice calling her name. She craned her neck to see where the call had come from, and a thick-set man with a dark hard hat and heavy industrial glasses emerged from the steam. He thrust a hand toward her.

"Harry Prysovich," he said, giving her hand a firm shake. "Otawnee High. Football team. Maybe you remember me."

Sharon studied the thick, work-roughened face before her. Harry Prysovich had been handsome in high school, a football hero. There was hardly a trace of his good looks left beneath the heavy flesh. He had been one of those who paid Sharon endless, finally almost bitter, court, and she had turned him down again and again.

"Harry," she said. "It's good to see you again." She nervously wet her lips, not at all sure what Harry's attitude would be.

"You're looking good. As good as ever," he went on with a grin. "Maybe better. I heard from the guys you did."

Sharon tipped her head in acknowledgment. "Thanks, Harry. You...you look good, too."

Harry laughed a single harsh laugh. "I put on some weight," he said.

Sharon shrugged sympathetically. "It's hard to avoid," she said. Her mind raced, trying to remember the roundly attractive girl Harry had dated when he had finally given up on her. "Did you and—"

"Lila," Harry said flatly. "Yeah. We got married. Got a kid graduating from Otawnee next year."

Sharon's mouth dropped open. "Next year? You're not serious!"

Harry shrugged. "I was a year older than you. We got married right out of high school. Kid's a junior now. Harry, Jr. Harry Junior's a junior." He laughed without amusement at his own joke.

Sharon nodded. "That's terrific, Harry."

"Yeah. Well, not so terrific. You know. Things don't get much better. I get up, I go to work, I have a few beers, I fight with the wife, I go to bed." His face brightened a little. "Play some softball, though."

Sharon looked at the jowly face before her, trying to find the high school hero. She remembered how she had treated him when she had known him before—not with intentional cruelty or arrogance, just without interest. And he had never really understood why, why she didn't think he was a hero like everyone else did. She felt a wave of sympathy. There was nothing evil about Harry; he wasn't even stupid. But he would never again find days as good as his high school football days.

"How about some coffee, Harry?" she asked.

Harry insisted on paying for both of them, careful to ask Sharon her preference about cream and sugar, then putting coins in the machine and retrieving the two Styrofoam cups. They walked slowly back to the side of the rolling mill.

The heat was tangible, shimmering in the air, but Sharon hardly noticed it. She had always loved being enveloped by the steam, and the way the hissing of water hitting the hot strip of steel shut out other sounds. They almost shouted to make themselves heard.

Harry talked about football. He could recall every single game he had ever played, and he could describe tackles he had made move for move. When he talked about football he was almost eloquent. His arms ranged in great arcs around his body, and his face had an intensity about it that drew Sharon in. She leaned toward him, avoiding his circling arms, her brow wrinkled in concentration.

Suddenly a body inserted itself between them. Mark Somers had a hand on Harry's chest, and his other hand clenched in a fist.

"What the hell's going on here?" Mark shouted.

Sharon stepped back, surprised and momentarily frightened. Harry's face showed bewilderment and then an almost instinctive anger. He batted aside Mark's hand and stepped away.

"Jeez, Mark, lay off. Can't I even talk to an old friend?"

Mark's eyes darted back and forth between them, finally settling on Sharon's face, which by now was registering her annoyance. He dropped his hands to his side. "So what *is* going on?" he asked, not quite ready to apologize yet.

"Exactly what Harry says," Sharon explained evenly. "A few reminiscences between friends."

Mark stuck his hands into the pockets of his corduroy trousers, pulling them taut across his hips.

"I'm...I'm sorry," he said, addressing himself to Harry. Then he turned and faced Sharon accusingly. "But after what you said this morning, about the possibility of some kind of danger, some show of hostility..." He looked back at the other man. "She seemed to think she might have some trouble after the newspaper article." He smiled and shrugged. "And you were waving your arms around, and Sharon looked so serious..."

There was a confused vulnerability about Mark's apology, and Sharon felt a sudden twinge of guilt. It *had* been her fault; she *had* exaggerated. And woven in with the guilt was a small but undeniable sense of pleasure. Mark cared. If he didn't care, why on earth would he have come rushing over to the rescue?

Harry looked back and forth from Mark to Sharon for a moment, his thick features showing a sudden, dawning comprehension. His eyes narrowed slightly, almost slyly.

"No problem, Mark," he said heartily. "Well, listen, I got work to do. See you, Sharon. Mark." He turned, cup of coffee still in hand, and headed back into the steam.

The slab on the mill track was cooling now, turning a soft, glowing yellow-gray as it banged its way back and forth, controlled by the almost invisible men upstairs at their computer screens. It had thinned out to an inch or so now, and it ran a hundred feet or more in length. The cooling water hitting it sent out less steam as the slab lost some of its furnace-induced heat, but the hissing and metallic clanging continued.

Sharon looked at Mark curiously.

"Really, Mark," she said banteringly as Harry disappeared. "Isn't it enough that you play mother hen to your workers? You really don't need to pull me under your wing as well."

The creases that cut across Mark's wide forehead deepened, and his mouth pulled into a small frown.

"Okay, love. Next time you're on your own."

He started to turn away, but Sharon put a hand on his arm. He had shed his corduroy jacket, and the sleeves of his shirt were rolled up to the elbow. She could feel the damp hair of his forearm against her palm.

"Mark . . . I'm sorry. It really was half my fault. I may have exaggerated a little this morning, and in any case, you seem to have been right about the men. There doesn't seem to be much problem. I . . . thanks for your concern."

Mark looked at her for a moment longer, then nodded thoughtfully. "Right," he said. "First you accuse me of breach of contract. Then you tell me I can't possibly have any understanding of the people who work here, despite the fact that I've been working here myself for eight years, because of some accident of my birth. And now, because of your little exaggeration, I almost started a fight with one of my employees. Terrific."

"Oh, come on, Mark," Sharon responded quickly. "Harry understands. It was just one of those things."

Mark nodded slowly, but his expression didn't change. "And you just want to be left alone to do your job. Well, so be it. I'll go do mine."

Sharon watched as he made his way back through the diminishing steam, his light-colored shirt still visible as far as the other end of the shed. She felt somehow forlorn, left behind. It was a feeling she didn't like at all.

Chapter 5

FOR OVER A WEEK, Mark was true to his word. Sharon
saw nothing of him except, on one or two occasions, his
back as he left a room the moment she entered it. For
several days he wasn't at the mill at all—in Pittsburgh,
Donna informed her when she casually asked. Sharon
told herself she should be happy, that Mark's behavior
was removing an unanticipated complexity from her return to the Otawnee Valley. But she didn't feel happy.
What she felt was an empty space inside, a space she
had never noticed before but that she now realized had
been there a long, long time.

She threw herself into the work. It was work she was
used to doing and loved to do, and whenever Mark's
face with its funny, crooked smile floated into her imag-
ination, she shooed it away with an effort of long-dis-
ciplined will. Even on the weekend, she spent time at
SomerSteel or working with her computer in the hotel
room, breaking now and then for a long drive into the
neighboring Amish countryside.

Then, at four in the afternoon of the Thursday of her
second week at SomerSteel, Mark pushed open the door
to her office. There was a wide grin on his face, and his

body was almost hidden beneath floppy work pants and a denim shirt.

The empty space inside Sharon filled up as if it had never been there. He stood in the doorway, waiting for her summons to enter the room, and Sharon felt her heartbeat quicken. The tingling she had come to recognize as Mark's distinctive effect on her was beginning to take hold. She nodded.

"Hello, Mark. Come in."

He sat on the worn couch and stretched his long legs out in front of him, his hands in his pockets. "So," he said finally, still smiling his almost silly grin. "How's it going?"

"Everything's fine, Mark, thank you."

"I've missed you," he said simply. "Insulting as you may be at times."

Sharon played with the pencil in her hands. She didn't know what she wanted to say: I've missed you, too; or, I'm sorry; or, please, please stay away. She felt the cool, professional shell begin to form around her, and she knew her instincts were providing their own, unbidden response. Her heart was beating so quickly she could hardly breathe properly, but the shell remained in place.

"So," he said.

Sharon looked at him expectantly. "Did you want something, Mark?"

His grin broadened, if that was possible. "You drive a hard bargain, love. I guess I wanted to apologize, or at least sort of explain. About why I flew off the handle about Harry. See, I've spent a lot of time getting in good with the Harry Prysovichs of this world. And suddenly there I was, about to punch him out. Harry Prysovich. I couldn't believe I'd screw up like that, just because I was in love. Especially after the things you'd said to me."

Sharon stared at him. "You certainly throw the word

love around easily," she said finally.

Mark shrugged but said nothing more.

"Would you really have hit Harry?" Sharon asked.

Mark's eyebrows rose. "Oh-h-h, yeah! And let me tell you, it would have been a disaster. Not smart at all. Big fellow, Harry is."

Sharon put down the pencil she had been holding, almost as if she were finally giving permission for Mark to stay.

"Okay," she said. "And I'm sorry for... whatever I said that offended you."

"Does that mean you believe me about the newspaper article?" he asked. "And you take back that other stuff? About my money?"

He sounded like a pouting little boy, and Sharon had to press her lips together to keep from smiling. There was no denying how good it felt to have him sitting here in her office, his pale, glimmering eyes focused on her face.

"I reported my unhappiness about the publicity to your father. That's all that needs to be done," she said in her best professional voice.

"That doesn't answer the question," he said.

Sharon folded her hands together. She had really almost forgotten the newspaper business. She *had* reported it to Byron, and he had promised to look into it, but she doubted he would. In any case, there had been no further problems from it.

When she didn't answer, Mark shrugged. "Anyway, how's it going?" he asked again.

Sharon glanced down at the papers on her desk. "Well, I've talked with about sixty percent of the employees and all but one of the officers. I've done some analysis of production figures and sales figures, and I've got a pretty good grip on what your needs are—"

Mark was shaking his head vigorously. "No, no, no,"

he interrupted. "Don't talk figures. I don't want to hear about figures. I don't even want to mention the word . . ." He paused, leaned forward, and mouthed "modernization." Then he leaned back again. "I want to know about Sharon Dysart. What's it like, being back in the Valley?"

Sharon opened her mouth, closed it again, and shrugged. "Modernization is why I'm here, Mark. It's no different from being anywhere else. It's my job, that's all."

Mark grabbed his chest at her words, as if he had been stabbed. Then, when she had finished, he lowered his head a little and looked up at her skeptically. His body formed a straight line, shoulders resting against the back of the couch, his bottom balanced at the edge of the seat, and his legs stretched out in front of him, crossed at the ankles. His hands were again jammed in the pockets of his grubby pants. His chin rested on his chest, and she could see the length and thickness of his eyelashes as he seemed to look up through them. He didn't say anything.

"Well, it *is*," Sharon found herself saying, as if in response to some unspoken argument from him. She picked up the pencil again and fiddled with it for a moment, then smiled in amused annoyance and tossed it at him.

"Oh, okay, so it's not. It *is* different. It's been . . ." Her brows came together in a little frown as she hunted for the right word. "It's been fun," she said finally. She blinked in surprise at what she was saying. It *had* been fun—except for the confusion Mark brought with him. "Everyone has been terribly nice, really, though God knows they have no reason to be. I . . . I didn't spend much time with them when I was here before, and I'm probably not going to do them much good now."

Mark nodded slowly and pulled one hand out of his pocket. He held it in front of him, making little circles in the air as if to say, "And then, and then..."

"Besides," she said in response to his moving hand, "I always liked this mill. It makes me remember why I wanted to work in steel mills in the first place. I like the heat and the way the air shimmers over the furnace and the river... I don't know."

Mark's smile had a certain satisfaction to it now. "So you like it here," he said almost smugly.

Sharon raised her chin a little defiantly. "Your turn now, Mark," she said. "What was it like for you, coming back here after you'd been away? Had you changed?"

Mark finally let his hand fall to his thigh and rest there. He shrugged, but he didn't answer, and Sharon felt a small, sudden shudder at his silence. If he *was* the same person he had been fifteen years ago, wouldn't he simply desert her again? Wasn't that the caution she'd been trying to implant in her brain for over a week now?

Sharon looked away from him, turning her chair a little so she could see the view out her window. There is nothing to desert, she told herself firmly. I'm a free woman, an independent woman; Mark Somers has no claims on me. Outside, beyond the window, the bright sunlight almost obscured the fiery glow from the strip mill.

"Have you seen any old friends besides Al? Oh, and of course, Harry?" Mark asked softly. "Do they seem changed to you, these people you left behind?"

Sharon turned back toward the room, folded her hands again on the desk in front of her, and considered his question. "No. I don't suppose they've changed. I may never have really understood them."

She looked up and smiled. "Of course before I was sure that *they* didn't understand *me*. Al Romanelli was the only one. I loved the mills, and that was just really...peculiar. You couldn't love the mills and be a woman."

Mark pulled his other hand out of his pocket and sat up straight. "Kids don't understand a lot of things," he said softly. "But I sure can't imagine anyone not thinking of you as a woman."

He was on his feet in one movement, his long body suddenly fluid as he rose. He held his arms in front of him, beckoning her, making a space for her, and she stood up as if he had pulled her up on strings. Her feet glided over the worn carpet as she moved toward him, and he folded his arms around her as she reached him, drawing her close.

Sharon felt a sudden, overwhelming flood of relief and pleasure, as though this was where she had wanted to be all her life, all these long years, and the space inside her, the empty space, was not simply full but overflowing.

"Oh, Sharon," he murmured in her ear, "I couldn't stay away any longer."

She slid her arms around his waist. They stood that way for a moment, looking at one another, studying each other. Sharon could see every twinkle of those sky-blue eyes—no gray in them now—and every nub of hair, almost red, around Mark's mouth and chin. She could see the freckle beside his left eyebrow, the tiny scar at the bridge of his nose where they had repaired the break, the gleaming dampness of the sandy curls that rested on the back of his collar.

"You've got gray in your hair, too," she said softly.

"Mmm-hmm." He lowered his mouth toward hers.

The day had been a little cooler than usual, and Sharon had pulled her window open a few inches earlier in the day, hoping to let a little fresh air into the office. Through that window now came the sounds and smells of the mill, the sounds and smells Sharon had always loved, had always wanted to be near. As her mouth met Mark's, she was dimly conscious of the unending breathing of the furnaces, the hissing from the strip mills and the constant, omnipresent heat, a heat that rose in great waves from the yards and the furnaces and the mills, a heat that seemed to have a life of its own.

She felt him against her, and she met his mouth hungrily, using first her lips and then her tongue to explore the sweet hardness of it. Her eyes closed, and she abandoned herself to the kiss, letting the urgency of it carry her forward as she pressed herself against him, fitting herself to his body as though she had always been part of him.

Mark pressed his hands against her back, and he slid them slowly over her hips. Wherever he touched her, Sharon felt the heavy heat of the air penetrate her flesh. The heat moved inward through her body in great waves, warming her, moving slowly, inexorably toward the very center of her sexual being. His hands touched her shoulders, and she felt the heat there; her buttocks, and she felt the heat there . . .

With the slightest pressure on her hips, Mark lowered them both back onto the overstuffed couch. Sharon settled against him easily, feeling the rough, worn fabric of his work pants against her legs. She let her shoes slide off, onto the floor.

Mark drew the sweetness from her with his mouth— from her cheeks, her eyelids, her eyebrows. Finally he let his lips trail lazily back to her mouth. His tongue toyed with her teeth, and Sharon met it with her own tongue, playing little games until the games became too serious, too urgent, and their tongues explored more deeply, thrusting inward, finding solace with one another.

The heat still moved into her in slow waves, moving inward from her shoulders, her back, her face—wherever his mouth and his hands touched—always just a little closer to the center, in a steady, rhythmic movement like the breathing of the furnaces. She shifted slightly next to him on the couch, and she heard him groan.

Mark lay back against the couch and pulled her to him. Her breasts thrust against his chest, almost aching now with the desire to be touched, and her legs stretched behind her on the old, worn cushions. Sharon could feel the dampness of his breath as he kissed her forehead, and she could feel the heavy beating of his heart through the fabric that separated them. One strong hand stroked the back of her neck; the other rested for a moment on her lower back, then moved slowly over the firm roundness of her buttocks.

She felt enclosed, safe. At her back, she felt the touch of his hand against her inner thighs, of his thumb as it caught at the edge of the silk cloth that covered her. Beneath her, she could feel the hardness of him against her belly. Her mouth sought his again with an almost lazy hunger, and she slipped her hands beneath his shirt, feeling for the first time the smooth lines of his chest, his sides, his back. He seemed consumed by the heat just as she was; he was throbbing with it.

A massive metallic crash broke through the heat, and Sharon's eyes blinked open. She sat up suddenly. Mark moaned and reached for her with both hands, but she curled into a corner of the couch.

Mark's eyes were suddenly wide.

"Hey," he said in a voice thick with excitement. "Sharon . . . love. What's the matter? Come on, love." He sat halfway up and touched one hand to her arm, but Sharon shook her head.

She stared out the window, at the office door, everywhere but at Mark. The heat had not quite reached her center, and now she felt it receding, like the tide that comes in and then goes out, deserting the depths of her, her belly, her heart, moving back to her edges.

"I'm . . . I'm not eighteen," she whispered, not even sure herself what she meant.

With a little groan, Mark pulled himself up until he was sitting and crossed an ankle over one knee, tucking his shirt back in where she had pulled it loose.

"Of course not, love," he said, a little frown playing at his forehead. "And I'm not twenty. And that makes it all even better."

Sharon shook her head. "No."

She couldn't think what else to say, what she could possibly tell Mark Somers that would make him realize how much she doubted him, how much she doubted herself. She had loved him—been infatuated with him— once before, partly because he had been handsome and fascinating, but partly because he had been Mark Somers. A symbol of what she had wanted to be. Was her attraction now the same thing? In confusion, she nibbled her lower lip.

It was the Valley. It was being back here, where she had been so miserable for so many years. There was something in the air; it was making her fall into old patterns again. And she had struggled so long and hard to leave it all behind!

She stood up and straightened her skirt.

Then, because it seemed like something he might understand, she said: "I can't afford to get involved now, Mark. I have lots of work to do."

She glanced at Mark and noticed for the first time how flushed his face was. The heat . . . But the flush was fading slowly now.

His eyes opened wide, and he jammed his hands into his pockets again, as he had when he had first sat on the couch. He nodded, then suddenly smiled.

"Well. Okay," he said. "Though it would make my life a little simpler if you'd make these decisions sort of . . . earlier."

He rearranged his legs, settling more comfortably into the couch. "We'll just wait until you're done. Which," he went on, opening his eyes even wider, "I'm sure will

be soon, since there's just not much to be done in terms
of modernizing here, is there?"

Sharon pursed her lips slightly. What caught her attention was the last part of what he was saying. The tone
was almost cajoling, as though he were holding out the
satisfaction of her attraction to him as bait, to get her to
admit the modernization job didn't need doing.

She felt wary again, and it wasn't just wariness about
her feelings for Mark. It was wariness about the sincerity
of everything he had done, everything he had said so
far. How could she keep forgetting what was first and
foremost in their relationship: that they were on opposite
sides?

She put her own hands in the pockets of her skirt and
began pacing in front of the couch, finally moving back
behind the desk.

"Actually," she said, "there might be some fairly major changes to be made. Computerization of a number
of aspects, continuous casting from the basic oxygen
furnace to the finished product..."

"Oh, boy." Mark looked up at her from the couch.
"Here we go again." Then suddenly he was on his feet,
too. "I can't believe you're really going to go ahead and
recommend that stuff," he interrupted. He stood in front
of the desk and put his hands down on it, pushing his
fingertips against its surface. There was nothing boyish
about him now. "How many jobs do we lose, Sharon?"
he asked in a quiet voice. "How many guys do you put
out of work?"

Sharon looked at him through narrowed eyes. She let
herself down into the big swivel chair and folded her
hands in front of her on the desk. "Well, of course some
slots will have to be abandoned, but..." Why was she
feeling cold in the midst of all this heat?

Mark clenched one hand into a fist and let it drop
harshly onto the desk. "Not *slots*," he said. "Not slots.

These are people, Sharon. *People*. Your father worked here. You should understand that."

Sharon smiled grimly. I know you, she told herself. I know you're no different from all the others, no matter how fiercely you insist you are. You want what you want, and you won't let anything stand in your way.

"Job loss will be minimal, Mark. You'd gain, in addition to an increased profit line, a more efficient and safer work place. I have trouble believing you'd turn all that down to save a couple of jobs."

He was staring at her, the silvery blue of his eyes glittering like ice. Only moments before she had opened herself to him—to his lips, to his heat. She had felt an unfolding inside herself that she hadn't felt since the first days of her marriage. Now she closed herself off again, shutting him out.

She straightened her shoulders and folded in on herself, as she had so constantly with Jean-Paul, as she had taught herself to do from the earliest years of her life. But no matter how carefully she pulled the shell around herself, she couldn't make her heart stop racing, nor could she control the tingling that flooded through her whole body, touching her very center, when Mark looked at her.

"Besides," she added coldly, "I can't remember that you used to worry so much about what happened to other people." It was calculated to hurt, and it did.

Mark jerked back from the desk almost as if she had reached out and slapped him. He folded his arms across his chest.

"If you're talking about our childhood fling, love, I've explained to you what happened then," he said, his voice even and, to her ear, slightly sad. "I know we disagree about what should happen at SomerSteel. I was hoping I could get you to see my way. Short of that, I thought we might share something outside the mill. But

I'm beginning to understand that there isn't anything for you outside the mill. So I guess I was wrong."

He turned and left the room. Sharon stared after him, watching as he pulled the door carefully shut, and the last of the heat deserted her body. She rubbed her shivering arms, then lay her head down on them on the desk. After a moment, she sat up again, pulled a stack of papers in front of her, and began to read. It was the only way she knew to forget the emptiness.

A little more than an hour later, Sharon packed up her papers and headed for her car. Al was at the gate. She pulled to a stop beside him, and he jumped to his feet and leaned both hands on the lowered passenger-side window.

"You must get here early and leave late!" he said, pushing his glasses up onto his nose. "I haven't seen you since your first day. Been hearing about you, though."

Sharon raised her eyebrows. "Oh? What's the word on me?"

Al shrugged. "Nothing much. Just that you're asking questions. Guys are concerned, but they're not scared much. Not yet. Oh, I did hear something . . ." He looked straight at Sharon and grinned. "Something about you playing around with the boss. Anything to it?"

Sharon met Al's gaze and held her own eyes steady. "Not a thing," she said evenly. "I'm too busy to play around with anyone. Besides," she added with a little shrug, "today was the first time I've even *seen* Mark in over a week."

"Figured it was just jealousy," Al responded. "Say, when can we get you over for dinner? Jeannie's dying to meet you. Did you see the newspaper article last week? You must have. She's on leave from the paper, because of the baby, so she couldn't put her name on the story. But when I told her you were here and why, she went back and found our old yearbook and did some research at the library and got all that stuff back downtown that same evening. She's quite a lady."

Sharon stared at him, wide-eyed. "You mean—your wife—your *wife* wrote that article?"

Al nodded so heartily his glasses slid down his nose again. His smile was proud. "I told her you might not like that high school picture. But isn't she something? She's been with the paper for five years now."

Sharon nodded her head slowly. "Yes, she must be something. Tell her thanks for me, Al. The article was just fine. And I'll live down the picture." She put the car in gear, a bemused smile on her face. "And the first part of next week for dinner, okay?"

"Anytime you can fit in it," Al replied, already opening his book and stepping away from the car. "Give us a call, would you?"

"Right." Sharon stepped on the accelerator and pulled away with a wave. Jeannie Romanelli. And she had been so sure it was Mark, even after all his self-righteous denials. A wave of relief swept over Sharon, a wave so huge and overwhelming it was almost tangible. Mark hadn't done it! And that was really where her mistrust had begun, over that damn article. Maybe...

He had said he believed they could have something outside of the mill, something beyond the way they felt professionally. Sharon wasn't sure, but at least there was the possibility of starting out all over again, with a clean slate. All it needed was an apology from her. That would be a beginning, anyway.

Back in her room at the inn, Sharon stepped out of her gray skirt and slipped the gauzy blue cotton blouse off her shoulders. She tossed her underwear, damp from the heat of the day, into a plastic bag to one side of the bathroom, then padded back into the bedroom and lay back naked on the bed. She closed her eyes in sensual pleasure for a moment, remembering the touch of Mark's hand on her flesh and feeling a little leap of flame deep inside at the memory. Then she reached for the phone book.

Mark hadn't been responsible for the article. That seemed wonderfully important, as though it made everything all right again. Sharon shifted her body against the pillows, enjoying the soft feel of the coverlet against her bare skin. Cool air from the air conditioner washed over the gentle rises of her breasts and her thighs.

She thumbed through the phone book to the *S*'s. There was the family mansion: *Somers, Byron, Park Lane.* Sharon pictured the house she had driven by once or twice, the great stone fantasy that stood at the end of its own private cul-de-sac. The property behind it—property that had once been the family farm and estate—had been donated to the town several generations ago and now was the site of a spacious town park, complete with a bandshell, small lake, public pool, and even a nine-hole golf course. Now the house stood on less than an acre of its own land, but that was almost an acre more than Sharon's house had had to itself. She smiled.

There were several other Somers listings, including one for Mark A. Sharon looked at it, puzzled. Maybe, she thought, there's another Mark Somers in town. Maybe *my* Mark lives at home with Dad. Certainly, she told herself, he can't live here: *4771 S. River Rd. #2, Otawnee.* She knew River Road. It was just a block or two from where she had grown up herself. It was not the kind of neighborhood she could possibly imagine a Somers, of *the* Somerses, calling home.

But perhaps, as Mark so often insisted, he really was different.

She dialed the Otawnee number. It rang again and again, but no one answered.

Chapter 6

THE PHONE WENT unanswered all evening. After bathing, Sharon kept trying, less and less frequently, until almost midnight, and then gave up. She wondered idly if it was the right Mark Somers, and where he might be.

By morning the need to apologize, the feeling that somehow an apology would start things off on the right foot again, had faded. After all, Sharon told herself as she dressed, what was there to start?

She put a toenail through her stocking and swore softly in annoyance. The truth was, there was plenty to start. And she might as well admit it. Her body started shaking and tingling every time the man came into sight. Sharon smiled wryly as she pulled on another pair of pantyhose.

She was used to facing things honestly; that was how she got along so well in business. And if she faced the question of Mark Somers honestly, there was only one, very frightening answer: She was in love. She was as head-over-heels in love as she had been years ago, but this time the physical infatuation was founded on something more—something shared in the way they both looked at life, something of hard lessons learned.

Sharon drove the half mile to the mill with the words

echoing in her head. She loved him. She loved the man who had deserted her years ago, the man who thought the work she did was all wrong. The man who would, in all probability, go to any length—even seduction—to discredit her. She batted one hand against the steering wheel as she turned into the yards. It *won't* happen, she told herself grimly. I won't let it happen again.

But she *did* owe him an apology. Mark wasn't at his office when Sharon checked, and the message she left with Donna that she was trying to reach him brought no response for the remainder of the day.

By midafternoon, Sharon felt the familiar protective coolness wrapping itself around her again. This time she was grateful for it. It was the shell Jean-Paul had found first amusing and then irritating, the shell that had turned his comments from teasing to sarcastic ones. Sharon let it fold her in; she found comfort in it. It helped her ignore the space that had opened up inside her all over again. She plunged into her responsibilities at the mill with a vengeance, and she used every atom of will to keep the image of Mark Somers's face out of her head.

It was Friday, and Sharon was grateful that the second week was about to end. One more to go, and then this job would be done with. And she would be gone. Away from here, where everything she did, every direction she turned, seemed to bring only more confusion.

But Friday was also the day she had agreed to accompany Byron Somers and his wife to a dinner-dance at the Somerville Country Club. When he had asked her, early in the week, it had seemed like one of those things Sharon had often done for the sake of her work: meeting the people in power in their own setting.

It had also seemed, she had to admit, like the final triumph of her return to the Valley. For a girl growing up ambitious in Otawnee, the country club had seemed the final fulfillment of the good life, the best of all possible worlds. She had to admit that she had been looking forward to it in a backhanded kind of way. But now she hardly felt like going through the moves.

Back at the inn after work, she lingered as long as possible in a warm bath, washing the accumulated grime of the day at the mill off her body, and she wondered idly what the inside of the club would look like. Not all that elegant, probably, she told herself dryly, compared to what she had already seen in her life.

She thought about the role the country club had played in her conversation with Mark on that first—only—evening, and she slapped at the surface of the water with her palm, scattering droplets of soapy film up the walls around the tub. The thought of that evening flooded through her all at once, like the heat that rose from the mill furnaces when the metal poured in, and the memories of Mark poured into the open space inside her.

Then she sat up abruptly, letting the water cascade away from her body. It was not the only evening she had spent with him, she reminded herself. There had been, after all, two evenings fifteen years ago. Sharon closed her eyes as she scrubbed herself with the soapy wash-cloth. For the first time since she had come back to Somerville, for the first time since she had seen Mark so unexpectedly, she let her mind travel back to those two nights, those two wonderful, seductive nights.

She could almost feel how she had felt then, when she had first realized that he was looking at her. She had been kneeling beside the basketball court at Somerville High, feeling, as she always had in her cheerleading outfit, a little silly and out of place. She had hoped, when she first became a cheerleader, that it might establish some common ground with the other girls, but it had only made her feel more separate.

So she had been kneeling there, a little apart from the others, and she had had that sensation at the back of her neck that someone was staring at her.

She had turned, finally, and there he was, the golden boy. Mark Somers. Sandy-haired, athletic, two years away at college. Staring at her. She had turned quickly back toward the court, but the sensation had continued. And every time she looked around, there he was, still watching her.

After the game she had lingered by the court, waiting. And he had come to her just as she had known he would, asking if she could see him the next night. They *had* been wonderful, those two nights. She could still feel the excitement of it, the nervous energy his presence seemed to generate in her, the way he had laughed and talked about college, the way it had felt to dance with him. His hands, only his hands, had made her realize what wanting was all about. And although nothing had happened, she had understood how it could, how one could want it to...

Sharon rinsed off and stood up, then rubbed herself dry with a thick towel and slung it over the shower-curtain rod. She ran her hands slowly down the sides of her own body. Her flesh was warm and taut to the touch, and her breasts came erect as she touched them lightly. It was a body that liked to be touched. If only...

Sharon shook her head. Yes. If only Mark Somers were a different person. And I were a different person. But we're not. And all the love I may feel for him won't change that.

She spent longer than usual dressing. She had brought the perfect dress—a long black and silver slip of a gown with padded shoulders and long sleeves, a dress that clung to her, moved with her every step, and showed off her slender body to its best possible advantage.

She was careful with her makeup and her hair, too, outlining her high cheekbones with plum-colored blusher and her large jade-green eyes with silvery-green shadow and dark mascara. She brushed her black hair until it glistened, then swept it up onto the top of her head, using the curling iron to make a jumble of thick waves. She studied the results critically in the mirror, added small silver earrings and a single jade ring, then smiled with satisfaction at the reflected image.

She was, of course, overdressed. As she entered the club with Byron and Charlotte Somers, the silver and black column of her dress with its New York sophistication drew every eye. Most of the women wore long plaid skirts and blouses that tied at the neck, or short, chiffony dresses. Sharon told herself that that was half the fun; everyone in the room would notice. No one would ever think of Sharon Dysart as the little girl from across the river again.

But the triumph was an empty one. She knew, when all was said and done, that whether or not these people respected her really meant very little.

And she was alone. As she chatted at dinner about life in Paris and New York, as she moved from partner to fascinated partner after the tables had been cleared, Sharon was overwhelmed by a loneliness that was stronger than she had ever felt before. She was thirty-three. She was lovely and successful. These were, for her, simple facts. But she was alone. She had abandoned her home, and she had never really found a new one—not with Jean-Paul, not in New York, certainly not here at the Somerville Country Club.

She wished suddenly that she were at a party in Otawnee—maybe at Al and Jeannie Romanelli's for dinner—wearing an old Indian-cotton dress, with her hair loose down her back. She wished for friends—and she wished for love.

Byron Somers cut in on the handsome, dull young man with whom Sharon had been dancing. Byron was as elegant a dancer as he was a dresser, and Sharon forced the wishes from her head as she followed his lead.

They chatted about the mill, and then, almost without thinking, Sharon asked, "Will we see your son tonight?"

Byron threw back his head and laughed. "Not likely!" he said. "Mark hasn't been here since his wedding reception, and that was something of a trial for him."

Byron paused for a moment, waving to a friend who waltzed by. "Mark spent half the time playing the piano with the band and the other half in intense conversation with . . . let me see. I think it was one of his shift foreman. He and Dana had made an agreement, I believe. He would let her have the reception here if he could invite whomever he wished. I don't think she expected to see half of the line workers at SomerSteel march through the door."

Byron chuckled, and Sharon looked up at his face. He was shaking his head lightly. "Neither did I, to be truthful. I knew right then that the marriage was in trouble, but it took Mark and Dana another eighteen months or so to figure it out." He looked at Sharon and winked. "My wife never did understand."

"No," he repeated after a moment, "I don't think we'll see Mark tonight."

But Byron Somers was wrong. When the dance was over and Byron led her off the floor, her gaze wandered over the crowd, and she saw Mark. He was just arriving, and he was alone.

Sharon drew in a sudden breath, almost a gasp. Mark was wearing a tuxedo, perfectly cut in classical style, with a simple white shirt, black tie, and the edge of a blue cummerbund showing below the last button of the jacket. His sandy hair glowed golden in the reflected light of the chandelier, and even from this distance, his eyes were distinctively blue. He looked smashing.

Sharon blinked, and her eyes followed him as he made his way slowly through the crowd. He hadn't seen her yet; he didn't seem to be looking.

She excused herself from the little group she was a part of and worked her way toward Mark. He was greeting everyone, and it was clear that people were surprised to see him here. Sharon hesitated to one side of the couple he was talking to, waiting for him to be free.

Mark saw her, and his eyes widened as they traced her figure from head to toe, taking in every detail, every rise and fall of her gown. Sharon's palms felt moist, and the pulse that always began when he looked at her sounded like thunder in her ears. He bowed from the waist.

"Good evening, love," he said, clearly amused. "Don't we look terrific tonight."

Sharon smiled in spite of herself and let her own gaze wander over Mark's tall figure. "Why, yes, we do," she said. Then she pulled her shoulders straight in a defiant gesture, but all she succeeded in doing, she realized, was making the dress cling more sensuously to her breasts. She folded her arms across her chest and looked at Mark as coolly as she could manage.

"I've been looking for you," she said. Her voice was a little testy, and Mark's eyebrows rose slightly.

"Have you now? I seem to remember a message or two. I'm sorry. I had a full schedule today."

"I tried to get you last night as well." Sharon pressed her lips together. She really hadn't meant to say that, to make her need to see him sound quite so petulant.

"Ah." Mark's gaze was steady, and his eyes were the same remarkable blue that she could see even in her dreams. "Well. I, uh, I didn't get in until rather late." He paused for a moment, then leaned his shoulders slightly forward, as if he were going on the offensive all of a sudden. "What was it you wanted to see me about?"

Sharon pursed her lips. He wasn't going to make this easy. "I've wanted...It's my turn to apologize," she said. "Al Romanelli told me that his wife had put that article in the paper. Apparently she works for the *Clarion*, but she's on maternity leave, so she didn't sign the material. I'm sorry I jumped to conclusions about you."

A small smile played around Mark's mouth. "Ah," he said. "So the great newspaper mystery is solved. The ever-efficient lady makes a mistake. Well, I expect we'll have to figure out an appropriate penance, won't we?"

Sharon took a deep breath. The blue of Mark's eyes was bright, almost blinding. Why did he have to look so incredible? It really wasn't fair!

"I simply wanted to say I'm sorry, Mark," she murmured.

Mark stretched out a hand and gently touched Sharon's cheek. He smoothed her upswept hair over her ear and touched her earring lightly. She could feel the impression of his hand on her hair, and she felt a shiver race through her. Then, with a feathery softness that surprised her, he slid one arm around her waist and grasped her hand with his other.

"Care to dance?" he whispered in her ear, but the question was a little late; the pressure of his hands had already moved them out onto the dance floor. His movements there were as smooth and elegant as his father's, but there was a strength about him that Byron didn't have.

"Do I have a choice?" Sharon followed his lead easily, letting her body glide lightly at his touch. She felt almost giddy, having his arms around her again. It was seductively treacherous, the way her body responded to his hands. And we're supposed to be annoyed with each other, she told herself wryly.

"I knew you'd been trying to reach me," he said after a moment. "Don't you want to know why I ignored your messages?"

"As long as I've made my apologies . . ." she began, although she *did* want to know.

"There were a couple of reasons. First of all, I went

out and got drunk last night, so I didn't get any messages at all until a little later than usual."

Sharon pulled her head away from Mark's shoulder and looked up at his face. There was an almost sheepish smile on it, but no more explanation was forthcoming.

"And then, when I did get in, I got told that good old Harry Prysovich managed to see me coming out of your office yesterday afternoon all hot and bothered. I assume you know that he spent most of last week letting it be known that you and I were a little more than friendly. And if that gets around and gets believed, it'll compromise my position with the men. So I thought I'd just go back to leaving you alone for a while. Make sure I didn't lose anybody's trust."

Sharon pulled away from him and stood stock still on the dance floor. "So you thought you'd just stay away from me until it suited you to come back. How charming."

"Hey, wait. I'm trying to be honest here." Mark reached one hand for her waist again, but she backed away. Suddenly all her doubts and fears were coming together.

"And of course *here* you're on your own turf. It's safe here. None of your precious mill folk are going to see us here, Lord knows." She clenched her fists at her sides. "You talk about what a humanitarian you are, Mark, but you haven't learned the first thing about how to treat people."

She spun on one foot and started away from him, but he caught her arm with his hand."

"Whoa," he said. He was smiling, and his smile infuriated Sharon all the more. "You didn't let me finish."

"I've heard enough, thank you," she snapped. "Last time you didn't want to compromise your position with your father, and this time it's with your employees. Well, just what's the difference? I'm not quite good enough for you in either case."

She started to turn again, but both of Mark's hands

closed around her arms. Sharon could feel their warmth
through the material of her dress.

Mark's voice was soft when he answered, but there
was a firmness in it, a determination that hadn't been there
a moment before. "You don't believe a word I say to you,
do you, Sharon? You just assume that anyone with money
is an insensitive lout. It's as though you can't see *people*,
Sharon. You just see cardboard cutouts."

Sharon opened her mouth, but Mark raised a hand
and touched his finger to her lips.

"Let me finish this time. You figure that when I came
back to the Valley, when I accepted my share of own-
ership of SomerSteel, I automatically took back on all
my father's attitudes and prejudices as well."

Sharon shook her head. "No," she said in a voice so
quiet it was almost a whisper. "I don't think you took
them back on. I think you never lost them."

Mark ducked his head abruptly, and when he looked
back at her his cheeks were flushed.

"You're the one who hasn't changed, Sharon. You're
the one whose perceptions have stayed the same, no
matter how far you've come and how much money you've
made. *I'm* not the one who thinks you're not good enough.
You are."

She stared at him. His hands still enclosed her arms,
but she knew instinctively that even the lightest shake of
her shoulders would dislodge them, and she could turn
and walk away from him forever. All she had to do was
take one step backwards, and Mark Somers would be
out of her life—again—as surely as he had been the
first time.

But she didn't move. She stood still, and his hands
remained. Slowly, he began to move them gently up and
down her arms, stroking their silvery covering, bringing
warmth to her.

She let her gaze drop to the floor. The pulse at the

base of her throat beat wildly, out of control. Why was she still standing here? Because, she told herself grimly, I love him.

"It's so confusing, Mark," she said finally. "Coming back here. Finding you here."

He nodded sympathetically, and his hands made little circles on her shoulders.

"I know," he said. "I did it myself. I came back, after I'd promised myself I never would." She glanced at his face, and he smiled. It wasn't one of his dazzling grins, but it was a little, ironic twist of his mouth. It was wonderful.

"Come on," he said then. "Let's get out of here. This place gives me the creeps. Let me show you what I'm all about."

Sharon wanted him to touch her, to hold her, to kiss her—and she wanted to turn and run away. "But you've only just gotten here," she said, playing for time, hoping her confusion would fade.

Mark just stared at her, his eyes shining blue in the light from the overhead chandeliers. Looking into his eyes felt like looking into one of the furnaces at the mill; they seemed to reveal a blinding fire down below, deep within him.

Sharon nodded almost imperceptibly. "I don't much like it here, I must admit. The club, I mean."

She touched a finger to her cheek, just beneath her eye, to make sure the tears that had suddenly threatened had not spilled over. Her cheek was dry. "I'll have to say my good-byes to your father and mother."

Mark laughed. "No problem. I'm sure someone will relay the message." There was an ironic tinge to his voice, and for the first time since they had stopped dancing, Sharon looked around them.

Not *every* eye was on them, she told herself, but it was close. Dancing couples glanced at them as they swooped by, and a small crowd at the punch table watched as they talked. There was no getting around the fact that they were the center of attention.

Suddenly Sharon felt a surge of mischievous energy.

"Right," she agreed. "Let's get out of here."

A few moments later Sharon climbed into the ancient VW and pulled the hem of her dress in behind her. "Any place special in mind?" she asked.

Mark turned the key in the ignition. "Home," he said firmly. "Like I said, I want to show you how I live. Maybe that'll help you understand me."

He backed the car out of the lot and headed down the hill. Minutes later they crossed the main bridge that separated Somerville from Otawnee.

"That address in the phone book *was* right," Sharon murmured.

Mark glanced at her sharply. "You didn't believe I'd live in Otawnee? I happen to like it over here." There was a touch of belligerence in his voice, as if he had told himself how much he liked it many times before.

He pulled the car to a stop in front of an old frame house, one of many old frame houses that stood almost against one another on a narrow street. The house had a front porch with one column missing, and the concrete sidewalk was treacherously broken. Noise from a television across the street penetrated the darkness.

Sharon looked around, eyes wide, as Mark took her arm and led her carefully up the walk, unlocked the front door, and pushed it open. There was a small foyer with three mailboxes, a staircase straight ahead, and two doors, one opening to either side, just in front of the stairs.

"I'm upstairs," Mark said. "There're two apartments down here, but I have the whole width of the house."

Sharon stopped on the first stair. Mark's hand was still at her elbow, and now she pulled her arm through it until her hand met his. She took hold of it lightly.

"Why?" she asked. "Why here?"

Mark shrugged. In the dim light of the staircase, Sharon could hardly see his face. "Because I wouldn't live in the family mansion."

"But weren't there some choices in between?" Sharon felt a wave of understanding for Mark that threatened to take her breath away. He had wanted out of his way of life just as much as she had wanted out of hers.

"Were there for you?" he responded. He turned and led the way up the stairs, letting his hand just hold the tips of her fingers. "If you were to move back here, wouldn't you want the biggest house, at the top of the hill—on the other side of the river?"

Sharon was silent in the darkness. It was true, as he said; his flight was really the mirror image of her own.

The room Mark let them into was a kitchen, small and rather drab, with one overhead light fixture. But, Sharon noted with a smile, there was a collection of electric "toys" on the counter, including a blender, a food processor, and a coffee grinder. Through the kitchen was a living room, furnished comfortably with an overstuffed couch and several chairs, and with books stacked on the floor.

Mark gestured at the room. "You wanted to know how I came to terms with all the money and power I inherited. Well, this is the answer. I stay as far away from it as possible."

Sharon nodded, but she felt a smile playing at the corners of her mouth. "But not quite so far that the stereo and the VCR get left behind," she said.

Mark spun around to look at her. He had switched on a small lamp by the sofa. For the briefest of moments, she thought he was angry; his pale eyes flashed silver in the dim light. But the grimace on his face was a comic one, and almost immediately he tilted his head back and began to laugh, running a hand through the curls that had been carefully tamed to agree with his elegant dress.

"Yeah," he said in mournful tones when his laughter had subsided, "I'm a fake. I guess it's true. I work so damn hard, and I'm so damn earnest..." His grin tilted across his face, making the tan seem even darker in contrast to the dazzling white teeth.

Sharon returned his smile. "Oh, come on, Mark. It's not the toys—I mean everyone on the line has what you have and more. It's..." She turned away from him, glancing about the room. Then she looked back to him again. "It's the sense of confidence you have, that innate optimism. You just radiate a feeling that everything can be handled, that *you* can handle everything. It's something the people I grew up with never had. Something *I* never had."

Mark's smile had faded slightly as he listened, and when she had finished speaking, he moved toward her. She almost instinctively held up both hands, palms forward, and he stopped where he stood.

"For me, what makes me different from those people at the country club is the way I have to prove myself to myself all the time," she continued. "*All* the time. I mean, nobody else really cares. I'm a success, in everyone else's terms. But I'm never quite satisfied. You were right about what you said back there, Mark. It's only me who still doubts me."

She shook her head, and she felt a warmth around her eyes where tears were beginning to well. "We carry our pasts with us, Mark, and I'm just beginning to realize that that's okay."

Mark took one more step forward, and he was in front of her. He lifted his arms and pulled her against him.

"I went out and got stewed last night because I thought I'd screwed up whatever chance I had with you, Sharon. I need you, love," he said, his voice husky. "I need you to tell me how dumb I am."

He buried his face in her shoulder, and his next words were a murmur so low Sharon almost didn't hear them. "Oh, Lord, you're the most beautiful woman I've ever seen!"

She could feel the warmth of his mouth against the side of her throat, and his sandy curls tickled her ear. She slid one hand around him, beneath his jacket, and raised the other one to his head, burying her fingers in his thick hair.

Somewhere deep inside, a small, warm flame was lit, like the first pilot on one of the great furnaces. Sharon could feel it just barely beginning, warming a single spot deep inside her, at the very root of her.

They stood that way for a moment longer, still, their bodies pressed together, and Sharon felt safer and more sure of herself than she ever had in her life. Then Mark raised his face from her shoulder and brought his hands up to cup her face, his thumbs gently stroking her cheeks as he studied her. His eyes were diamonds in the evening light, blue-white and glittering with heat and desire.

Slowly he lowered his mouth toward hers, and Sharon felt the tiny flame leap inside her. It seemed to lick at certain nerve endings, now on the inside of her forearms, now at her thighs, now at the base of her throat. His mouth moved closer, and she opened hers to him, as if in a dream. Sharon heard a moan and knew it had come from somewhere inside her, somewhere that the flame now raged.

His tongue explored her mouth lazily. They had all the time in the world, and she could taste the sweetness of him with her own tongue as it moved over his lips, his teeth, the inside of his cheeks. There was a tiny aftertaste of champagne about him, from a drink at the club, and something vaguely smoky. Then the slow laziness disappeared before the onslaught of the ever-widening fire inside her. It was deep in her loins, urging

her toward him, and she could feel the hard heat of him
through her dress.

He broke away from her. With one strong movement,
he scooped her up in his arms and carried her through
an archway and into his bedroom. Sharon felt no desire
to resist. The only desire she felt was for Mark, to feel
his smooth skin against hers, to bring him to her.

"Oh, Mark," she heard herself murmur. "Oh, yes."

She stood beside the bed where he had gently set her
down, her arms at her sides. His hands held hers tenderly.
They studied each other, drinking in each other, as though
every feature were new and extraordinary.

"I've wanted this for fifteen years," Mark whispered
hoarsely. "And I think you have, too"

Sharon could only nod silently. Just moments earlier
she would have thought the remark arrogant, but now it
seemed the simple truth. The fire had moved through her
now; she could feel its raging heat in her cheeks, in her
belly, in the firm but vulnerable flesh of her breasts,
whose dark centers felt engorged with it as they pressed
against the fabric of her dress. Her breath came in small,
shallow gasps.

Mark stepped behind her. She felt his hand against
her back as he unzipped her dress, and his fingers as he
let them trail along her warm flesh. Then his mouth
followed, tracing a soft, moist pattern down the line of
her back where the zipper stood open all the way to where
it ended, just at the swell of her buttocks. Sharon felt
the pressure of his lips there, and a shudder raced through
her. Everywhere his mouth touched, the fire followed.

With strong hands, Mark slid her dress off her shoulders, rolling the long sleeves down off her arms. The
dress was so perfectly cut that she had worn no bra, and
now she stood naked from the waist up. Only the moonlight from the two large windows lit the room. Sharon
crossed her arms across her breasts, and she could feel

the taut flesh at their centers against her forearms. At her back, his hands still at her waist, Mark kissed her bare shoulder.

He turned her around to face him. His hands felt soft and warm against her hips, and his eyes explored every exposed inch of her. Sharon felt somehow both there and not there. The touch of his hands was as intense a touch as she had ever experienced, almost burning, and yet she felt at the same time detached, as if she were standing to one side, watching these two people find each other. The air around them seemed to shimmer with heat, as it did by the mill on a hot summer afternoon. Her body ached with wanting him.

Sharon met his gaze steadily. He was still fully dressed, and after a moment she reached forward and slid his jacket off his shoulders, letting it fall to the floor. With slow, studied motions, she untied his black bow tie, reached behind him to unsnap the cummerbund that circled his waist, then unbuttoned his shirt. It seemed to her that her hands must belong to someone else; the fingers moved so carefully, without a single wasted movement, but what she felt inside was something chaotic, overpowering. The heat was so intense inside her now that she felt almost faint from it; the fire was licking into every corner of her being.

Sharon's fingers fumbled at his cuff links, and Mark pulled them out himself, then slid his shirt off and dropped it onto the floor on top of his jacket. Her eyes consumed him, the planes of his smooth, naked chest, but she did not touch him. Instead, she folded her arms again across her own breasts. The flames had become an ache, an almost rhythmic ache that moved through her in great waves of heat, invading her most intimate, hidden spaces.

Suddenly Mark moved behind her again. He worked the slim silvery dress over the swell of her buttocks and hips, down her thighs, and let it fall to the floor. Tenderly, he slipped his hands inside the band of elastic that held her final silken wisp of clothing in place. She could sense rather than feel him as he knelt behind her, slipping the fragile material down her legs. She closed her eyes. Her breath came in short, labored gasps as she stepped away from the clothing that now lay at her feet.

Mark stood and reached around her; he put the palms of his hands flat against her belly and pressed against the soft, ivory flesh, pressing her back into him. Sharon let her body rest against his, feeling the smooth strength of his chest against her back, the sandpapery roughness of his thighs, and the naked, swelling hardness of him against her buttocks. She put her hands behind her, on his bare hips, liking the feel of bone and sinew beneath her palms.

He moved his hands softly over her belly, and his fingertips grazed the dark hair just below it. Sharon shivered at the sudden surge of heat in her body. He slid a hand up her breast and let his thumb play lightly with the dark, erect center, teasing it, making it fill his palm. His other hand burned at her thighs, finding her moist center, and she closed her eyes in exquisite pleasure.

Then the flames leaped through her with an irresistible intensity. With one abrupt motion, she twisted around in his arms and pulled him to her, pulling them both back onto the bed.

Like a fire seeking oxygen, Sharon's mouth and hands explored every part of him with desperate urgency—the wide shoulders, the smooth planes of his chest, the flatness of his belly, and the line of thick, almost red hair that descended from it. Her fingertips glided over his body, pressing here and there, wherever she felt the warmth of his desire for her.

The fire inside her wanted to consume him, and her tongue transferred heat from her body to his, to the rising flesh of his nipples and the tender flesh inside his elbows, to the pulse at his wrists and his throat and at the base of his belly. Mark sent the flames back to her, his mouth caressing her breasts, her shoulders, her thighs, until they could each no longer breathe. And then, finally, he fit the length of his body to hers and entered her, came to her in great, rhythmic thrusts, like the almost molten ingots on the track, crashing back and forth, back and forth, glowing orange and red with their heat until a shower of fireworks exploded inside her, and then the flame slowly, inexorably, began to recede.

Chapter 7

WHEN THE FLAMES had finally been extinguished, Sharon nestled back on the big bed, exhausted, and pulled the sheet up over herself. She let her eyes wander about the room, seeing for the first time the random stacks of books, the Ben Shahn print tacked on one wall, the framed posters she recognized as being from the labor movement of the 1930s. It was obviously a functional room, used for reading and sleeping. It was not designed, Sharon thought with a smile, to entertain visitors.

Mark lay on his side, supporting himself on one elbow. He traced the outline of her face with his other hand, letting his fingertips linger over her cheeks, her mouth.

"You know," he said thoughtfully, "I can hardly remember what you looked like fifteen years ago. It's almost as if I was blinded then, by your . . . radiance. Or something." He smiled.

Sharon let her eyes rest on his face. "Maybe you never saw me at all," she said softly. "Not really. Maybe I was just a . . . something you could fight your father with. A cardboard cutout, I believe those were your words."

"Ah, stabbed by my own rhetoric," he said, pulling

an imaginary dagger out of his chest. Then he rubbed one cheek thoughtfully, considering the proposal. He shook his head.

"There was that in it, of course," he said. "But there's also no denying that I thought you were the most beautiful creature I'd ever seen. I wanted to see you every minute. I couldn't understand how I hadn't noticed you all those years, when we'd played Otawnee—I figured you must have been just as mesmerizing in sixth grade as you were in twelfth."

Sharon smiled as she lay back against the pillow. Mark hooked one finger under the sheet and pulled it down, uncovering the soft, ivory flesh of her breasts. "Just the way you are now," he said with a shake of his head. He touched one nipple lightly and watched, intrigued, as it hardened and darkened.

Sharon pulled the sheet firmly up again. "I'm not sure the superstructure was quite the same in sixth grade," she said. Then she rolled her head to one side so she could see his face. "And are you blind now, too?" she asked. Her tone was teasing, but the question was important. She wanted him to assure her that he saw her now as she really was—and that she was worth fighting for this time.

Mark flopped over onto his back and laughed. "My goodness, no. I see you flaws and all this time. All your insane hard-headedness, and the way you turn yourself on and off. And I think you're terrific anyway."

Sharon could see only his profile. The wide, lopsided grin was in place, and he was making little shadow figures with his hands against the ceiling in the light from the single bedside lamp.

"Is that what you think?" she asked. "That I'm hard-headed? That I make myself cold and hot whenever I feel like it?"

Mark glanced at her for a moment, then looked back

at the ceiling. "Duck," he said, gesturing at the shadowy outline with his chin. "Very hard to do."

Sharon looked at him steadily. He waggled his hands, and the duck flopped over.

"Dead," he said. "Or maybe just in heat." He looked at Sharon and grinned. "See? Like me." He bounced a little on the bed. Sharon lay quietly beside him.

He pushed himself up on one elbow again and ran his other hand through his tangled curls. "Actually you're doing it right now, you know. You've turned into the professional lady again. Cool and calm. Despite the unusual attire."

Sharon closed her eyes for a moment, then lay back against the pillow. He didn't understand, not really. Not for all his professions of sensitivity. He didn't understand that the coolness that seemed to settle over her so often was something she had created long ago, for protection, and that it now came, unsummoned, unwanted, even when she no longer felt need of it. He didn't understand how frightened she still was of his love.

"Why did you come back to the Valley, Mark?" she asked finally. "If you hated it so?"

Mark shrugged one shoulder. "My uncle died and left me half-interest—almost, anyway—in the corporation. By that time I'd worked for a while in the mills out west, so I figured I knew what the problems were. I figured I could come back here and maybe do things right. Instead of just watching the profit line."

Sharon studied the ceiling where Mark was once again making shadow animals. "You *have* done something right, you know, Mark," she said. "You have a good mill. And everyone likes and respects you."

"Oh, yeah. I've worked hard at that part of it." He folded his hands together in the air. "Walrus," he said. "One of my prize numbers." He wiggled his little fingers, and the walrus waved its tusks.

"But I made a few mistakes along the way," he went on. "For instance, my late, unlamented marriage. My high school lady was still around and still single. I think my father had kept her informed, and she figured she'd wait it out. So we just sort of drifted together again. About as good a reason to get married as yours was." He pursed his lips slightly, in something between a smile and a grimace.

"Dana. A delightful lady. The banker's daughter. Turned out she thought she was marrying my father. When I told her I actually wanted to spend time at the mill, where I was employed, she couldn't quite grasp it. She thought we should be playing tennis."

Jean-Paul's face, handsome, charming, then finally bitter, drifted through Sharon's mind. "Was it...unpleasant?" she asked, remembering the icy battles with Jean-Paul.

Mark laughed again. "Oh, no. Very civilized. She divorced me and married some magnate down in Pittsburgh. She wanted to move on to bigger and better things." He rolled over onto his stomach and gazed steadily at Sharon. "Sort of like you."

Sharon felt a sudden chill, as if the fires that had raged just a short while earlier had been reduced to a pile of almost cold ashes. Yet the ashes proved the fire had been real.

She reached over and pulled the pillow from his side of the bed and swung it against his head.

"I am *not* a gold digger," she said with mock indignation. But there was no denying that the remark had hurt.

As Mark pulled the pillow out of her hands, she sat up and slid her legs over the edge of the bed, and his return blow glanced off her back.

"I've got to be on my way, Mark," she said, keeping her voice light. "I..." She turned on the bed to look at him where he lay. The features of his face were so appealing that she almost gathered him in her arms again. But she didn't.

The intensity of the passion they had shared felt overwhelming and confusing. Did he really love her? He used the word so casually, all the time.

Everything was happening too fast. A man she had thought she loved years and years ago and whose leaving her had colored her life since then had suddenly reappeared, and now she thought she loved him again. No, she told herself as she stood up, I *do* love him. She had to have some time to sort out the muddle.

"I can't possibly be seen coming back to the inn tomorrow morning in *that!*" She gestured at the elegant silver and black striped dress where it lay in a little bundle on the floor. "I mean, if you're concerned about what people are saying!"

"Love, I no longer give a damn."

Mark reached an arm over her, but Sharon stepped away from his hand. She stooped over and scooped up Mark's dress shirt from the floor and pulled it around her.

"No," she said. "I have to get home, Mark."

"Home," he repeated thoughtfully. "To the Otawnee Inn. Nice to have room service at home."

Sharon glanced at him, acknowledging the joke, then gathered up her own clothes and headed into the bathroom to dress.

Waking up the next morning in her room at the inn was easier than Sharon had expected. She felt charged with a new energy, some new fire inside her—a remnant, she told herself wryly, of her adventure with Mark the evening before.

She wasn't sure how she felt about what had happened between them. There was no doubt that she had enjoyed it—more than she had ever enjoyed making love before. It had been like fireworks, like . . . like the mill, she thought with a smile. Just like the mill.

But Mark was still, despite last night, something of an unknown quantity. In some ways she knew him so very well, but in others . . . He had left her once before. His motives for seeing her then were, by his own admission, not entirely straightforward. And his motives now were equally obscure. Maybe he really did love her, as she, admittedly, loved him. Or maybe he was using her again. If he could discredit her work by bedding down with her . . .

Sharon scrubbed at her face with the hot washcloth, destroying the last traces of makeup left over from the evening. The silvery dress was packed carefully back in its plastic bag, and her hair hung loose over her shoulders, just a hint of curl remaining in it. With deft fingers, she pulled it forward over one shoulder in a thick rope and braided it, letting it fall straight down her back when she was done.

She stood for a moment longer in front of the bathroom mirror, examining the image she saw in front of her.

Mark had said she was beautiful. It was something she had heard many times, and she had used it to her advantage. But she had never thought of it as something special, something radiant. Only something useful. She stroked her cheek thoughtfully with the fingers of one hand.

A thick pile of papers lay on the desk in the bedroom, and Sharon glanced at them as she came out of the bathroom. The problem with all these unexpected complications, she told herself ruefully, was that they got in the way of the work she had come here to do. Too many distractions. She looked down at her body as she slipped off the light nightgown she had slept in. Too many distractions, she repeated.

But steel mills were always working. The furnaces would be burning on a Saturday, and, she told herself with a sigh, she might as well work, too.

The heat of the summer day was already gathering outside the air-conditioned room; Sharon could see the brilliant sun through her window. She pulled open the closet and reached for a tan skirt, then, on an impulse, hung it up again. She scooped her suitcase from the floor of the closet, unzipped it, and pulled out a pair of flat sandals she had had made in Greece some years before and a thin, almost diaphanous Indian-print cotton sundress. They were clothes she hardly ever wore anymore, but she always kept them at the bottom of her suitcase when she traveled.

If I have to work on Saturday, she thought, at least I'll be cool.

She let the dress settle over her. It hung from two slender straps over her shoulders to just below her knees, a swirl of blue and white print, and it felt good against her body. She was tired of the carefully conservative suits she usually wore for work.

Besides, she told herself with just a touch of defiance, I'll probably be the only management person down there. So what does it matter how I dress?

She did seem to be the only one in the administration building. The ancient air conditioning creaked and groaned in competition with the fierce heat outside, and every time Sharon turned over a page or did a calculation, Mark Somers seemed to be looking over her shoulder or stroking her hand or simply standing before the desk, his lopsided grin in place, watching her. His presence haunted the room as surely as the heat. Finally Sharon put her pencil down and her feet up.

Am I really as far gone as all that? she asked herself, bemused. Have I fallen all that hard? And the answer, she knew, despite her own vehement denials, was yes. Mark Somers had entered her life for the second time, and he had captured her heart just as surely as he had the first. She shook her head in dismay.

He had been so tender, so confident last night. But he had never said anything about the future. He had never implied that there would be anything more between them than . . . than the fire they had shared.

And if he had, Sharon wondered suddenly, how would she have felt? Could she live here, come back to the Otawnee Valley and be happy?

She shook her head. "I haven't been asked," she said aloud. "So just calm down, Sharon, and do your work."

By early afternoon the air conditioning had given one last wheeze and stopped functioning altogether. Sharon stood and stretched. She was hungry and hot, and her body felt tender, even slightly sore, from her exertions of the night before. It was hard to believe how long it had been since she had made love. She could feel the tiny, exquisite aches in her breasts, in her thighs, inside her where the flame had first begun. It was as if her body had come suddenly more alive; she could feel the heat and the sun and smell the smells of the mill just a little more intensely than she had yesterday.

She shook herself, letting the loose dress fall around her in folds. She worried for a moment that she should have worn a bra, and she fussed with the dress for a moment, making sure it covered her as completely as she knew it did, then she headed out into the yards.

She really didn't expect to see anyone in the little vending-machine room at the hot strip mill. The hand that touched her shoulder as she put money in the sandwich machine took her by surprise, and she whirled around.

"Mark?" The name was out before she knew she had said it.

Harry Prysovich had a sour smile on his face. "No, sorry to disappoint you, Sharon. It's only Harry."

Sharon smiled with forced friendliness. "I don't know why I thought it was, Harry. How're you doing? I didn't know you worked the weekends."

"Yeah, I work the weekends."

Harry just stood in front of her, not moving, like some mountainous part of the earth, just watching her. Sharon gestured at the machines nervously.

"Want something?" she asked. She held up the ham and cheese sandwich she had just pulled from its little compartment. "I'm having lunch. I'm starving."

Harry nodded slowly. "Yeah, I bet you are. Probably never can get enough, skinny lady like you."

Sharon heard the double meaning in his words and ignored it. "How about some coffee?" she said, turning away to put coins into another machine. She glanced up at him as hot coffee spilled into the cup in her hand.

Harry shrugged and finally smiled. He pulled some change from his own pocket and fed the machine. "Want to sit down?"

Sharon nodded. "Just let me get some sugar in this." She pulled the wrapper off the sandwich and dropped it into the trash, then stirred a packet of sugar into the coffee.

They sat facing each other at one of the tables, smiling a little uneasily. The end walls of the small room were lined with vending machines, but the two long side walls were glass from waist height to the ceiling, so anyone inside had an easy view of the thirty-six-inch strip mill. Sharon watched the figures outside the glass as they, in turn, watched the slab on the track move back and forth. The steam seemed a little lighter today than it had been several days before.

"So, enjoy the dance?" Harry asked. "Pretty fancy stuff."

Sharon blinked. "News really does get around." She

shrugged and looked steadily at Harry. "It was okay. It was part of my job. I went with Byron Somers."

"Ah." Harry nodded slowly, looking at her from beneath half-closed eyelids. "With Byron. That's not the way I heard it."

Sharon leaned forward on her elbows, chewing slowly on a bite of her sandwich. She felt a coldness in her stomach that didn't jibe with the heat of the air around her. There was something in Harry's voice that sounded unpleasant. "Just what did you hear, Harry? And from whom?"

Harry laughed. His fleshy face shook slightly with the sound. "Buddy of mine plays in the band for those dances. Said you came with Byron, but you left with Mark."

Sharon swallowed the bite she had been chewing and washed it down with a sip of coffee. The coffee did nothing to dissipate the coolness she felt inside. She was angry, but she tried to make her smile warm and friendly rather than—what was the word Jean-Paul had used? Imperious. Rather than imperious.

"It's remarkable how everybody knows everything in towns this size," she said as lightly as she could manage.

"Oh, yeah. You're used to bigger places. New York, Paris. I almost forgot." Harry took a big swallow of coffee and then leaned forward, across the table, so that his face was very close to hers. "So you finally got what you wanted, didn't you?" he said softly.

Sharon leaned back a little instinctively. "I don't know what you mean, Harry." Her smile felt painted on.

Harry reached a hand to his face and took a heavy fold of flesh in his hand, rolling it between his thumb and fingers. "Oh, come on, Sharon. You know exactly what I mean. Do I have to spell it out for you?"

Sharon looked at him stubbornly, silently.

"You got the boss. Just like you always wanted. You got the boss in the sack."

Sharon stood up so suddenly she knocked the rest of

her coffee over, but she hardly noticed. The heat of the mill seemed to have settled in her cheeks; they were flaming.

"I don't need to listen to this, Harry," she said, her voice steely calm and quiet.

Harry stood up, too, and Sharon realized what a big man he was—as tall as Mark, and much beefier. Thoughts raced through her head, and one of them was: I wonder if he's as strong as he is big. She glanced quickly toward the door, calculating how many steps away it was. Then she straightened her shoulders. Don't be silly, she told herself. This man is an old friend. He's not a threat.

"Nah," Harry said, more loudly now, "you don't need to listen. You never did listen before, not to any of us guys. Why start now? None of us was ever good enough for you, Sharon, not a single one of us guys. Were we? Huh, were we?"

Sharon could feel herself pulling in, pulling the shell around herself. She knew that the expression on her face right now would only reinforce whatever Harry thought she was, but there was nothing she could do about it.

He reached a hand across the table toward her, toward her shoulder, but Sharon moved a step sideways and his hand brushed her breast instead. The gathers of her dress shifted so only a single layer of thin material remained in place, and she knew that the outline of her breast must be clearly visible to Harry now. She felt a momentary surge of annoyance with herself for having picked this particular day to wear this particular dress, and she leaned forward and shook her shoulders letting the material fall into gathers again.

Harry shook his head. There was a half-smile on his face that was almost smug. "So now you trot back here, making a spectacle of yourself all over the mill, and start making time with Mark Somers," he went on. "Well, that's one way to get more jobs, baby. Just crawl into bed with the boss."

"You're being offensive, Harry." Sharon's voice was almost a whisper. What he was saying had never been true before, but now . . .

"Well, you were damn well gonna get out of here, and I guess that's one sure way to do it—sleeping with the guys that hire you. So let me just ask you one more thing, Sharon baby. Are they good? I mean, you think these guys are all that much better than what you turned down on the way up?"

Two things happened at exactly the same time. A movement caught Sharon's eye outside the long window that looked out onto the mill, and she reached across the table and slapped Harry across the face. The second was an instinctive motion, entirely without thought, and the moment it had happened she regretted it.

But in the time it took to raise and lower her arm, she realized what she had seen outside. She had seen a figure looking in through the window, and then turning away. The figure, she knew without thinking, was Mark Somers. She had no idea if he had actually seen the slap or not.

Harry Prysovich blinked and raised a hand to his cheek. He was looking at Sharon curiously, almost forlornly, as though he knew he had made a bad mistake, and as though he were used to the feeling.

Sharon looked at him almost blankly for a brief moment. "I'm—I'm sorry, Harry," she blurted. Then she turned and rushed out the door of the lunchroom into the mill corridor. Her breath was coming in quick gasps, and she knew that, if she let herself, she would cry. She would not, she promised, let herself.

Outside, in the mill, she hurried around the outside of the vending-machine room to its opposite side, where she had seen Mark. But he was no longer in sight. There was only the hard gray structure of the rolling mill and the soft gray steam that enveloped it, and all around the figures of men—dwarves—scurrying in the steam.

She stood a moment longer, peering into the steamy dimness of the mill. Whether or not he had seen her slap Harry, he had to have seen that she was in trouble, and he had turned away. After last night. She let a dry smile touch her lips, but she felt no amusement. Her hands, clenched at her sides, buried themselves in the folds of her dress, and its soft, filmy material felt cool against them. He had turned his back on her.

Obviously what Harry Prysovich thought of him was more important to him than what *she* thought of him, despite what he had said last night about not giving a damn. He valued his position among his employees more than he valued whatever he felt for her—if he felt anything at all. Sharon moved almost blindly back toward her own office. He had seen Harry reach for her, had seen that they were angry, and yet he had turned his back on her.

The tears she had refused to let fall made an ache against the back of her eyes. Harry's words rang in her head, and suddenly they seemed true. Maybe we're both using each other, she thought. Maybe he wants to make me give up my plan to change his mill, and maybe I want to prove I'm finally good enough for him. But even as she thought it, she knew that nothing could change the fire she had felt last night. No matter what her reasons, her love for Mark was real.

She locked her office door and walked, almost ran, to her car, heading up the hill to the inn through the Saturday afternoon shoppers. The phone was ringing when she entered her room, and she took two steps toward it, then stopped. It rang nine times. When it finally stopped ringing, she went to it and unplugged it from the jack. Then she sat down at the desk and did what she always did when she was upset: buried herself in work.

A knock made Sharon raise her head. At first she wasn't quite sure where the knocking sound was coming from; she looked absently out the window, where the sun was beginning to lower and streaks of orange and purple were beginning to appear. She was surprised at how late it was, and she remembered with a smile the beauty of the sunsets here, where the fading light filtered itself through the heavy smoke and particles sent into the air by the mills. Even pollution, she told herself dryly, has its redeeming points.

Then the knock sounded again, louder this time.

She rose and started toward it, then, as she had with the phone, stopped.

"Who is it?" she called.

"Come on, Sharon, give me a break. Open the door. I need to see you." The deep, musical voice paused, then went on. "I have presents," he said cajolingly.

Sharon hesitated a moment longer.

"Sharon, have pity! If you don't open the door, I'll make a scene, and the guy who manages this place will throw me out! Think of the embarrassment!"

A smile played briefly at her lips, in spite of her best efforts to keep it away. She moved to the door and swung it open. Mark stood there, a heart-shaped box of candy in one hand and a bouquet of flowers in the other, and an expression of bewilderment on his face so endearing that Sharon had to work at not reaching out to stroke his cheek.

"Can we talk?" he asked, like a little boy. "And can we start with why you're not answering your phone?"

Sharon pressed her lips together. "I'm trying to work," she said firmly.

Mark narrowed his eyes. "Fat chance, love," he said. "Not good enough." He took a step into the room.

Sharon stepped in front of him. "I don't know that you've been asked in," she said evenly.

Mark looked at her, and his eyes widened again. "Sharon, what the hell's going on? I didn't expect to see you at the mill, but when you turned up, I went to your office. It was locked. So then I started trying to call you here."

He looked around the room, took in the phone sitting, wrapped in its cord, on the bed, and nodded.

"So I had to figure I'd made you mad somehow, but it beats me how. You know, love, you gotta stop doing this kind of thing to me. First I go out and get publicly drunk, and now you have me tooting around the inn carrying—"

Suddenly he held out the gifts, as if just remembering them. Then he looked straight at Sharon, and he smiled. It was one of those wonderful, off-side smiles, and Sharon could feel her resolve melting just a little bit more in the face of it. "Do you have any idea how hard it is to find a heart-shaped box of candy in July?"

Sharon looked at the box of candy and at the flowers. The box was vaguely dusty, as though it might well have been on the shelf since Valentine's Day. She felt a little giggle rising in her throat, and she fought to control it.

"Thank you, Mark," she said as evenly as she could manage, taking the flowers and candy from him.

"That's better." He reached for her shoulder, but Sharon stepped away. He was charming; his charm confused her.

"I think we need to talk, Mark. Someplace neutral."

His eyebrows went up again. "So. I *did* do something. Okay. How about dinner downstairs?"

Sharon nodded. "I'll have to change."

"Oh, no, you don't," Mark cried, catching Sharon's arm in his hand. "I mean, you looked incredible last night, in that silvery thing. But you look every bit as wonderful today. Maybe even better. In sandals and a sundress. It's not everybody who could pull that off, love." He was grinning broadly.

Sharon looked at him. If only she could stop her pulse

from racing whenever he came near. If only she could not feel the surges of heat deep inside.

"Mark," she began and then stopped. She shook her head sharply, but the muddle remained. "Let's eat," she said finally.

They settled themselves at a corner table and ordered. Mark put their menus carefully one on on top of the other and folded his hands on the table.

"Now then. Can I find out what I did?" he asked.

Suddenly Sharon had a clear vision of this afternoon's scene again in her head: of Harry, big and fleshy and sour-looking, on the other side of the table; of Mark, outside the window of the lunchroom, watching, just watching. The anger and hurt she had felt then flared again, and she pressed her lips together.

"You didn't do anything, Mark."

Mark rolled his eyes. "Sharon, Sharon, Sharon. What am I going to do with you?" He leaned forward and rested his chin in his hands. "Please, love, let's not play games. Not after..." He winked and leaned even closer. "Last night," he whispered. Then suddenly he sat back again. "Or do you mean I didn't do anything last night? My love, if my performance wasn't good enough for you..." He shook his head in disbelief.

"Last night was probably a mistake," Sharon said grimly.

Mark's grin faded. "No," he said. "I don't believe you mean that. I want to know what happened *today* to change what happened last night."

Sharon was silent another moment. Then she said quietly, "You saw what was happening with Harry Prysovich in the lunchroom. I saw you outside. Why did you stand by? Is Harry's respect more important to you than my..." Her voice trailed off into silence again.

Mark's eyes opened wide, and he simply stared at her. She could feel the warmth entering her cheeks under his relentless gaze. Then, abruptly, he laughed.

"That's it?" he said. "That's the reason my *persona* is *non grata* around here today?" He shook his head in disbelief.

The blue of his eyes glittered in the light from the single candle on their table. "I didn't come to your rescue today, love, because I practically got my head bitten off when I did just that last week. If you'll remember. I figured I oughta take you at your word. You wanted to fight your own battles. I can't be expected to know when the instructions change unless you tell me about it."

Sharon blinked. It hadn't even occurred to her that the scene must have looked, from outside the window, identical to the one that had taken place earlier in the week. She opened her mouth, then closed it again.

"Well," she said finally, "it must have been clear when I slapped him that something more than a friendly chat was going on."

"Slapped him?" Mark had been rocking back in his chair, holding the edge of the table with his hands. Now he let the chair drop back onto all four legs. "You didn't! You slapped Harry Prysovich? One of your basic giants?"

Sharon ducked her head and nodded.

Mark whistled softly. "Something a lot of folks have been dying to do for a long time. Poor old Harry. Never quite gets anything right. Well, let me shake your hand, Ms. Dysart."

He reached across the table and gave Sharon's hand a quick shake, then turned it over and folded his other hand on top of hers. Sharon slipped her hand out from between his; it felt warm from his touch.

"What *was* old Harry saying, anyway?" Mark asked.

Sharon looked away. She had almost forgotten Harry's words, the stinging words that had precipitated the slap. Now they came back to her full force.

"I . . . I don't know," she muttered. "It wasn't anything important." He had said she had slept her way to the top. She knew it wasn't true, but in a way...She thought of Jean-Paul, the doors his name had opened for her at the very beginning of her career. But once they were opened, I was the one who walked through, she told herself defiantly. And yet still, now here she was, with Mark Somers...

Mark reached toward her and tipped her chin up with one finger. "Not good enough, love. What made you so mad that your famous cool escaped you altogether?"

Sharon stared at him steadily, silently.

"Ah. Stubborn. Let me guess. He said you were sleeping with the boss." Sharon tried to keep her face without expression, but something must have moved—a muscle in her cheek, an eyelid fluttering—because Mark grinned.

"Bull's-eye," he said.

"How did you know?"

Mark shrugged. "Because that's what he's been saying around the plant all week. Nothing new in that. Besides..." The grin widened and turned just a little wicked. "Now it's true."

Sharon frowned. "It's not something I do as a matter of course," she said.

"Ah. Is that what he was implying?" Mark nodded sagely. "So that's why the slap."

Sharon picked at the food on her plate with her fork.

"You really are good, you know, love," Mark said thoughtfully. "You're a joy to watch work. It's too bad all that energy and discipline couldn't be applied to something other than destroying people's jobs."

Sharon's head snapped up, and she put her fork down carefully beside her plate, waiting. Mark leaned forward, his chin on his hands and a good-natured smile on his face.

"You know, our comptroller is retiring soon. A matter of weeks. Why not chuck this stuff and come work for SomerSteel? Handle our money for us? Heaven knows, you'd be good at it. Efficient budgeting seems to be a real prime principle with you."

Sharon could feel the skin tightening on the backs of
her arms and along her neck. Could he really be offering
this, after she had made clear what her work meant to
her? Or was he buying her off in yet another way? Suspicion took root and almost immediately sought out all
the space inside her. He had offered affection, but she
was still steadfast about doing her job. So now he was
offering money—even a long-term employment com-
mitment. And one was no more important to him than
the other.

Sharon folded her hands on the table in front of her.
"I have no interest in handling your money for you," she
said, a steely edge to her voice. "All I'm interested in
doing is making steel as efficiently as possible."

Mark picked up a napkin and tossed it impatiently
back onto the table. "Efficiency isn't the be-all and end-
all of business, Sharon," he said. "If you can get approximately the same product at approximately the same
rate the old way, why change it? Just to save money?
We've *got* money. Why lay off workers in an area that
already has fifteen percent unemployment? Why don't
you . . ." He hesitated, and then a coaxing smile settled
on his lips. "Why not come back to the Valley, Sharon,
back where you belong. And do something that doesn't
involve throwing men out of work?"

Sharon wiped her lips carefully with her napkin and
then folded it and set it down by her plate. "I don't belong
here, Mark. Maybe I don't belong anywhere. But in any
case, I'm getting a little tired of being told what a monster
I am all the time," she said finally. She could hear the
coldness in her voice, and this time she didn't try to mute
it. She pushed her chair back from the table. "And if
you'll excuse me, I have work to do. Figuring out new
ways to pad the unemployment lines."

She rose and turned away from the table, not even
looking to see if Mark had watched her go.

Chapter 8

SHARON STOOD QUIETLY in the center of her room, wondering what had gone wrong. Where had she made her mistake? Was it in trusting Mark Somers for a second time in her life? Was it in falling in love with him all over again? Or was it simply in coming back to the Otawnee Valley, something she had promised herself never to do?

Her unhappiness fell loosely about her, like the cotton dress that still hung in gathers from her shoulders.

The love she felt for Mark was rich and all-consuming. It wasn't simply a matter of who he was, or what he looked like. Although, she admitted with a smile, she did love his wayward grin and his broken nose and his cherub's curls. She glanced at the heart-shaped box of candy on the bed. She loved his almost unflappable good humor and his compassion.

And he had said he loved her. Said it several times. He threw out the word *love* like a ball he was playing catch with. But still he didn't trust her to do her job with compassion equal to his. Still he was trying in every way he knew how to buy her off.

Sharon walked slowly to the big bed and carefully lay down on it, as if she were folding something fragile into layers of tissue paper. Everything about her felt brittle, slightly damaged, scorched, perhaps, by the flames of the night before. She pulled the thin cotton of her dress around herself and closed her eyes.

What was it Mark had said downstairs? Essentially what he had been saying all along: that modernization and efficiency weren't ends in themselves. That you had to think about the people.

Well, I *do* think about the people, Sharon told herself fiercely. She rolled onto her stomach and punched at the pillow with one hand. I *do*. Faces moved through her head in quick succession: Al Romanelli, Harry Prysovich, the boy who had sat at her lunch table that first week, her father . . . And Mark Somers.

Suddenly Sharon sat up. But maybe I *don't* think about the people—not in the way Mark does. In quick steps, she moved to the bathroom, slid the cotton dress over her head, and pulled her robe around her, violently knotting the tie at her waist. Maybe I don't, and maybe, just maybe, I can do it his way. She glanced at her watch. Only nine-thirty. Plenty of time.

She sat down at the desk and flicked on the computer, feeding it information at a steady, efficient rate. It had never been done before, modernizing a plant without putting anyone out of work. The common wisdom was that it *couldn't* be done. But she had seen parts of SomerSteel that could actually use *more* personnel, and if the slots could be coordinated with some retraining, with attrition, with enhanced flexibility of job descriptions . . .

It was after midnight when she finally switched the computer off, and the eerie green glow of the monitor screen faded slowly away. Sharon rubbed her eyes with her hands. The challenge was impressive. But if she could get a more precise feel in the next week of exactly who was capable of what at the SomerSteel Number One mill, it seemed just possible. The problem now would be time. Because this kind of a plan demanded that she know the skills and potential of each employee. It had to be personalized to a much greater degree than anything she had attempted before. And she only had a week.

But if she could do it... Oh, if she could only do it! The adrenaline was still surging through her body as she untied her robe, slipped on a nightgown, and climbed into bed. She was exhausted, but she was wide awake. She lay in bed, staring at the ceiling. Wouldn't Mark Somers, she thought with a wide smile, be happy.

Then, abruptly, another thought entered her head, and it took her by surprise. *I'll* be happy, too! If I can make this job happen this way, it will make me happy. Maybe for the first time in my life.

The next morning felt more like autumn than mid-summer. There was a wonderful snap in the air, a breeze that promised to blow the stale air of the last few days out of the Valley and replace it with something new and fresh. Sharon rose late and threw the window open as wide as it would reach.

She pushed the PRINT switch on the computer and let her calculations of the night before feed through the printer while she showered. By the time she had pulled on jeans and a red tunic top, a pile of paper as thick as her hand lay on the floor. She flipped through it with one finger, then let the papers fall back on themselves again.

In the light of day—even such a promising day as this one—some of Sharon's energy-induced optimism had faded. She looked at the figures on the print-out nervously. She felt far from sure that what she was pro-posing could actually be accomplished.

Or even if she wanted it to be.

Something nagged at her mind, and finally she admitted to herself what it was. Wasn't she doing this, trying to do this, just to please Mark Somers? Jean-Paul had wanted her to doctor figures to make his semi-legal moves look legitimate, and she had refused. Now here she was again, juggling figures for a man she thought she loved. In this case it certainly wasn't illegal, but didn't it amount to the same thing? She was succumbing to Mark's priorities, not her own.

She glanced at the papers one more time. But, she told herself, it *would* be a challenge. The muddle in her head was overwhelming. And besides, the day was much too nice to be wasted indoors. She restacked the printout and headed outside.

It was after eleven. The main street leading downtown was lined with churches and, at this hour on a Sunday morning, crowded with church traffic. Sharon drove down the hill slowly, her eyes flicking over the sidewalks crowded with families. She remembered the Sundays of her own childhood. Church with her father, midday dinner at . . . She smiled, thinking of the restaurant she had gone to the very first night with Mark.

It was open. Sharon zipped her little rented car into a parking space in front of it and went in. The homemade doughnuts were every bit as good as she remembered them, and the coffee was perfect. She sipped it slowly, reading over a copy of the Youngstown Sunday paper she had picked up at the front door.

People came and went, and every time the door opened, Sharon looked up. She smiled dryly as she realized why. It was possible that the someone coming in the door might be Mark Somers. But there was no Mark, only churchgoers in their Sunday best, extended families of several generations, coming in for Sunday dinner. Sharon felt a little shiver of nostalgia. Twenty years ago, she and her father would have come through that same door, hungry after the long morning service.

She downed the rest of her coffee, folded the newspaper, dropped a few coins on the table, then paid her bill at the front counter. Back in the car, almost without thinking, she headed over the bridge and into Otawnee. It felt as familiar as if she had never left. A left, another left, a right...

The house was still there. It was pale green instead of white, and it was in need of paint—something that had never been true when she and her father had lived there. But the yard was as lovely as ever. Whoever occupied the house now had the same green thumb her father had had. She smiled to herself as she pulled the car up to the curb in front of it. Roses in their prime sent climbing stalks up the walls on either side of the door; asters and zinnias formed a glorious mass of pink and purple down the sides of the concrete walk.

Sharon climbed out of the car and stood for a moment, leaning against it, looking at the house. Almost immediately a tiny girl, perhaps two years old, appeared around the side and then ducked into the front door, and a moment later she reappeared in a young woman's arms.

Sharon nodded. "Hi," she called. "I used to live here." She started up the path, but the woman just stood on the concrete porch, waiting. "My name is Sharon Dysart."

Suddenly the woman smiled. "Oh, yeah. You're Mr. Dysart's girl. The one who went away. I'm Sheila Duffy. Used to be Sheila O'Mara. We lived around the corner."

Sharon blinked. "Of course. You couldn't have been more than...six or seven when I moved away."

"How long you been away?"

"Fifteen years." Sharon felt a sudden heaviness inside as she gave the figure. Fifteen years. Long enough for Sheila O'Mara to have grown up and raised a family.

"I was eight then."

Sharon nodded again. "I'm just back to...to do some

work. I sort of wanted to see how the house was."

The woman turned and looked at the house, as if she hadn't noticed it lately. "Needs painted," she said. Sharon smiled to herself at the western Pennsylvaniaism—the dropped "to be" after "needs"—that she'd been hearing ever since she'd gotten back. Until then, she hadn't heard it in fifteen years. "Jamie hates painting."

"The garden looks beautiful." Sharon made an arc with her arm, taking in the green grass and the flowers and the roses.

Another face appeared behind the woman, a little boy this time, about five. He held on to his mother's knee with both hands.

"Jamie likes it to look nice. I think he'd really rather be a gardener than work at the mill, if he had his choice." She paused and smiled a little wanly. "Maybe he'll get it. They keep laying people off around here. But he puts in the hours over the weekend. Not much for TV or anything like that. I like my stories in the afternoon, but I work on the garden, too, when there's a chance."

Sharon nodded at the jumble of information. She was always amazed at the freedom with which people talked about themselves—even the men, in her interviews at this mill and at others. Here was a woman whom she didn't know at all, but about whom she knew a remarkable number of facts: that she liked her soap operas, that she gardened when she could, that she had a husband who loved gardening, liked his house to look nice, and didn't much care for watching TV.

It was odd how open people could be. She thought of herself, and how tightly she guarded information about herself until she was sure the listener could be trusted. Only Mark Somers had broken through that defense, had learned things about her on that very first evening that she rarely told anyone.

"Like to look around inside?" the woman asked.

Sharon shook her head. "That's okay. I don't want to bother you. But I do think I'll walk around a little. Will the car be okay there?"

"Sure." The woman shrugged. "If you think it needs watched, Timmy'll do it."

"Oh, no," Sharon answered. "I won't be gone long."

She looked at the house again. It was straight-sided, two-storied. Except for the flowers, it wasn't charming or picturesque in any way. But neither was it bleak, as she remembered it. There had always been flowers, and the house itself was narrow but solid, with three sturdy rooms on each floor.

She shook her head almost sadly. Why were there so few memories in her head of the good times, the long afternoons in the yard with her father, the sounds of children, the smell of roses?

A shrill whistle cut through her thoughts. Noon. She drew in a deep breath, and instead of the sweet smell of roses, what entered her lungs was air momentarily heavy with the thick, acrid smoke of the mill. A smile played around the corners of her mouth. Not bleak, but not altogether wonderful, she reminded herself. Even with antipollution regulations.

Sharon turned and, with a quick good-bye, moved on down the street. She walked in what seemed to her random patterns, down this street, up that one. Halfway down one block she stopped in front of a stone church and sat on the low stone wall in front of it. A service was letting out, and she found herself nodding hello as people came by—men and women she had interviewed at the mill, a waitress from the Otawnee Inn—faces she had come to know in the last two weeks.

As she sat, she turned over in her mind the plan she had begun to develop the previous night. It would have to be taken in slow steps—not at all the kind of plan she was used to drawing up. The modernized mill would eventually need less personnel, and that could only be accomplished through attrition. There couldn't be any pressure put on people to take early retirement unless they really wanted to. For the present, she would have to envision a system for the mill that would employ virtually everyone who was currently employed. She wondered dreamily if Jamie Duffy might rather take on some landscaping responsibilities, if that could possibly be worked out.

A landscaped steel mill! Sharon laughed to herself. What on earth am I coming to?

The last couple drifted out of the church and down the sidewalk. It was quiet, with only the muffled sounds of the mill hanging softly in the air. The acrid odor had blown off, and the day smelled fresh and crisp.

Sharon stood up. She felt energetic and determined. It was *not* a simple case of giving in to Mark Somers. He was right: These people were individuals. They went to church and ate Sunday dinners in restaurants, and suddenly, fiercely, she knew that she didn't want to put a single one of them out of work. Not even Harry Prysovich.

And the exciting thing was, it could be done.

She rubbed her hands together briskly. Mark would be as excited as she was. Without even a second thought, she set off to cover the five blocks that separated her from the street where she had been two nights before.

She turned into Mark's street and then, abruptly, stopped. What if, once he had gotten what he wanted from her, Mark's interest simply disappeared? What if . . .

Sharon shook her head sharply. Enough what-ifs. Enough second-guessing about peoples' motives. If Mark felt anything for her at all, this would only make him happier. And if he didn't . . . Well, she would weather that storm when it appeared.

She moved resolutely on down the block toward the

gray house with the broken sidewalk, hardly hearing when a voice suddenly called her name. She glanced quickly up and down the street, but there was only a handful of children playing hopscotch.

"Sharon! Up here." This time it was unmistakably Mark's voice. She looked up at the second-story window of the house. He was leaning out, his torso bare in the midday sun, watering a windowbox of petunias.

She smiled instinctively at the picture. "Hey, Mark! Getting some sun, are you?"

He patted the flowers tenderly, like a father patting his children on the head. "Gotta take care of my babies."

He ducked his head inside and then back out again, this time without the watering can in hand. "So, couldn't live without me?"

The children playing up the street looked at Sharon curiously. One of them, a boy of about ten, called a greeting to Mark.

Sharon felt the familiar tingling in her fingertips as she looked up at Mark, and she shook her arms to try to get rid of it. His curly head was outlined by the bright sun, and the golden-red down on his chest and belly were plainly visible against his deeply tanned skin. Even from this distance, his blue eyes glistened.

Sharon's cheeks felt warm, and she brushed a hand across one as if to brush away the color she knew was gathering in it. She searched unsuccessfully for some bright retort to his remark.

"Come to read me a poem, have you, love?" Mark called. "Or maybe a serenade?"

"Hey, Marko," the little boy yelled. "You gotta girl-friend?" And his friends all began to laugh the raucous, self-important laughter of children who have discovered a secret.

Mark leaned out even farther from the window. All he seemed to be wearing was a pair of jeans, and the sun made little pools of glistening light on his bare chest and back. Sharon's breath quickened, and she felt the pulse in her throat begin to bang harder and harder. He was sitting on the windowsill, his whole torso outside the window, balancing with one hand against the frame wall of the house. He moved the hand, jerked forward slightly, and grabbed for the windowsill again with a little yell.

"Mark!" Sharon cried in sudden alarm. "I'll come up!"

The kids laughed even louder. A girl, apparently sympathetic, came a little closer. "Don't worry, miss," she said. "He does that all the time. It's a joke."

Sharon looked at her for a moment with wide eyes. "Ah," she said finally. "Right." Then, with another quick glance over her head at Mark, she strode up the path and into the foyer of the house, then up the stairs, two at a time.

Mark was at the top of the stairs, leaning against the doorjamb. He had pulled a white shirt on but hadn't had time to button it. It hung loose down his sides, and the wide, smooth chest that showed seemed even tanner for the white that surrounded it. He had his hands in his pockets.

"Hi there, love," he said softly as she approached.

Sharon felt strangely shy. All that tan flesh confronting her, and the grinning face...She took the last few steps slowly. She could hardly remember why she had come here. She only knew that where she wanted to be more than anyplace in the world right now was nestled against that beautiful chest, with those strong arms wrapped tightly around her.

Still, she might have recovered herself if Mark had simply kissed her. She might have remembered what she was there to tell him. She might have shared the kiss and then moved away, full of her plans for the mill. But he didn't kiss her.

As she reached the top landing of the stairs, he stepped toward her, pulled his hands out of his pockets, and took one of her hands in his. He stood facing her, holding one hand between his two, and then gently, with great care, he placed her palm against him, holding it to his belly, just above the top of his jeans. There was a pulse beating there so strongly that Sharon, suddenly almost faint, wondered why she couldn't hear it drumming in the quiet air.

Mark moved slowly backward through the open door of his apartment, and Sharon followed, as if mesmerized, her hand feeling the heat of his body, his two hands folded over hers. When they were inside, he took one hand away and reached around her, pushing the door shut and then sliding her shoulder bag down over her arm.

He led her slowly back through the kitchen and into the living room. Sharon watched his eyes. They remained constant and steady on her own. The blue of them was like no blue she had ever seen before. It was translucent, it was like the sky, it was brilliant, it was like the ocean. She took in a deep, shaky breath. She had no idea why she was here, except for this.

His eyes still searching hers, Mark moved her hand slowly downward, inside the waistband of his jeans. She could feel the rough hairs that began there.

"Mark," she murmured. The thought had crossed her mind that this shouldn't be happening, that there was some other reason for her coming to him; but the word came out a sigh, almost a moan.

He unzipped her jeans. Falling slowly to his knees, he slid the jeans down her long, smooth legs. Her tunic clung to her hips, and he slid it upward with his hands, keeping them there at either side of her waist while he buried his face against the firm flesh of her stomach. She could hear his breathing, harsh and shallow, and she took handfuls of tangled hair in both her hands, then let herself slip slowly through his hands to her knees as well.

Sharon felt as though her senses were at once heightened and numbed. The nap of the carpet beneath her knees seemed to cut into them, but she felt no wish to move or even to shift her weight to relieve the discomfort. Mark's hands were warm and strong as they softly stroked the sides of her body, over the lines of her ribs. She could feel the separate touch of each finger against her taut flesh.

He took hold of the hem of her tunic, and Sharon raised her arms over her head, helping him free her of her clothing. The fire from the last time—the first time—was beginning to burn again. But now it felt controlled, as though she somehow held the key, the pilot, in her hand and could raise the flame slowly, never letting it flare until she—they—were ready.

Mark rocked back on his knees and pulled her against him. Her breasts, covered still by a fragile wisp of silk, were crushed against the smooth, muscular planes of his chest, and Sharon thought she could feel his heart beating.

He pressed his mouth against her shoulder, and she shuddered slightly at this first touch of his lips. Then, her hand wrapped in his tight curls, she raised his head to hers and met his mouth hungrily with her own. Slowly she let the flames rise higher. Her tongue flickered against his teeth; her teeth nipped at his lower lip; her hands, inside the waistband of his jeans, moved down over his hips.

Suddenly it was Mark who could wait no longer. A husky moan escaped him as he slid her underthings off over her long limbs, then hurriedly pulled off his own jeans. With an intensity that was almost frightening, he rolled onto his back on the carpet and pulled Sharon on top of him.

Her hair, hanging loose, washed over them both like a waterfall, and she wrapped her arms and legs around him, folding him into her, making a haven to protect him from the world outside. The flames leaped suddenly, unbidden, and everything inside her was an inferno again, a great furnace burning out of control. There was a throbbing, an ache at her very center. It was a pain so rich and exquisite that she cried out in the joy of it, and the empty space that seemed to come and go inside her was suddenly full, sated, engorged with his love.

For a moment afterward she stayed motionless above him, wrapped about him. Then, slowly, she slipped off him and lay on her side on the carpet.

Mark lay on his back, his eyes closed.

"My God," he said softly. Then he opened his eyes and grinned his lopsided grin at the ceiling. "My God," he repeated, louder this time.

He rolled onto his side, planted one elbow on the floor, and rested his head against his palm. He looked at Sharon through half-closed eyes. "How can I ever thank you?" he said with a slow shake of his head.

Without waiting for an answer, he fell back onto his back and beat both fists against the floor beside him. "Yahoo! Unbelievable!" he yelled.

Sharon looked at him, half amused and half horrified. "Shh," she whispered. "Whatever will the neighbors think?"

"Who the hell cares?" He raised his arms straight up and contentedly rubbed the back of his head against the carpet.

Sharon sat up and pulled her knees against her chest. For the first time since she had entered the apartment, she felt her thought process had returned more or less to rational. It was, she was suddenly and uncomfortably aware, one o'clock on a Sunday afternoon, and she was sitting naked on the living room floor of a man whom she had known for a total of three weeks of her life.

"Mark..." she began.

He sat up, too, and crossed his legs. He was smiling euphorically at her. "Yes, love. Speak to me."

"This hardly seems the proper time or place at this point..."

"Or attire, no doubt."

Sharon nodded. "Or attire. But I did come here to talk to you about something."

He turned the corners of his mouth down into a frown. "And not for my body?" he asked in a hurt tone.

Sharon opened her mouth, then closed it again. She couldn't keep the smile away from her own lips. "Well, that wasn't my intention," she said.

Mark looked back over his shoulder, as if there were someone behind him, as he had done that first day in her office. "She sounds so serious," he said soberly. "You don't suppose she wants to say something about..." He cupped a hand around his mouth and whispered, "Modernization?"

Then he turned back to her and rested his hands on his knees. "You will probably never have a more enthralled listener, love. I'm all ears," he said with a smile.

Sharon let her eyes rake quickly over him, then took a deep breath and let it out slowly. "Not quite *all* ears," she said.

Mark chuckled. "Don't remind me," he said. "You'll never get the talking done."

"Maybe we should—"

"Get dressed? Good idea." He stood up in one quick motion, retrieved his jeans from where they lay on the floor beside him, pulled them on, then gathered up Sharon's clothes as well and dropped them unceremoniously into her lap.

"Thanks," she muttered, head bowed in a sudden rush of embarrassment. Still sitting on the floor, she pulled on her underwear and jeans and tunic.

Mark disappeared into the kitchen. "You eaten?" he called.

Sharon nodded. "Yes. More or less. I had breakfast at Maria's."

"Ah." Mark reappeared in the kitchen doorway, grinning. "Doughnuts, no doubt. And you didn't even bring me any."

"I—I didn't know I was coming here, Mark. I *wasn't* coming here," she added more firmly. "I came over the bridge to see my old house, but then—"

"You were drawn to my side by some force beyond your control." Mark had moved out of sight again, and Sharon could hear the little buzzing sound of coffee beans being ground and the small whoosh of water beginning to boil.

She stood up and followed him to the kitchen doorway. "Actually, I've been working on something that I thought might interest you," she said, the excitement of her new direction slowly coming back to her.

Mark stood with his back to her. "Mmm," he murmured, fiddling with the coffeepot. "Always back to business. You're really incorrigible, you know, Sharon."

His back was broad and almost intimidating, and his voice sounded vaguely petulant, as though he were just a little annoyed. Then he turned, coffeepot in one hand and a cup in the other, a wide grin on his face.

"Let's forget the mill for an hour. Two hours. A day. Let's just sit and drink coffee and look into each other's eyes."

Sharon smiled, but she felt the beginning of a steely edge inside her harden a little. If he refused to listen, even now . . .

"We *have* to work out this business about the mill, Mark. It'll sit and fester between us if we don't."

"So. I *offered* you a solution about the mill. You quit

this modernization junk and come be our comptroller. But you walked out on me. I really don't see any other answer. Coffee?"

Sharon shook her head impatiently.

He poured out one cup of coffee, put the pot down, and took a sip. He was leaning back against the countertop in the dingy kitchen with its ripped linoleum and cracking plaster. He had pulled the white shirt back on, but it was still unbuttoned.

"Sharon . . ." he began in a soft, almost coaxing voice.

Sharon held one hand up, palm forward, to stop him. "Just what *were* you offering last night?"

Mark's eyes widened in surprise. "A job," he said. "Exactly what I said." Then he narrowed his eyes into a mischievous expression. "I promise I'd be the perfect gentleman. No strings attached."

Sharon smiled in spite of herself. "In that case," she said airily, "I'm certainly not interested."

Mark put down the cup and, still grinning his offside grin, took one step forward. He leaned his face toward hers for a kiss, but Sharon stepped sideways and rested her shoulder against the doorjamb on the other side, avoiding his mouth.

"No, really, Mark. I've been thinking and thinking, and I've about decided—"

"I don't want to hear it!" Mark interrupted. "I truly, honestly, don't want to hear how you've figured out how to cut only forty jobs instead of eighty. Please, Sharon . . ." He reached out a hand and let it rest on her shoulder. "I can't believe that after fifteen years I've gotten another chance at you. This time I don't want to lose you. If you'd take the job, you could have me, too."

Sharon blinked. She was amazed to find herself thinking rationally, confronted with that particular offer—and that particular bare chest. It was, she told herself wryly, *quite* an offer.

"For how long?" she heard herself asking, and her voice sounded cold and hard-edged even to her. "For two nights? Until you realize one more time that the real Sharon Dysart isn't quite so important to you as whatever your image of me is? Or until you've got me so irrational that I promise never to try to change your precious mill again?"

Mark stepped back and put a hand to his face, as if he had felt the implied slap. He shook his head slowly. "Come on, Sharon," he said in a voice that was almost a whisper. "Give me a break. I've told you what happened the first time. And you can't begrudge me trying to save something I've spent eight years putting together, making up for mistakes made by generations of my family before me. Why can't you trust me, love? Why can't you believe me?"

Sharon looked down at the floor. She *did* believe him. That was what frightened her. It would take no effort at all to step into his arms, to accept whatever he had to offer. But if she were wrong, if he left again...She thought suddenly, briefly, of Jean-Paul, who had seemed what he was not, and had seemed it so very convincingly.

"Mark, come to the mill with me. Right now," she said. She knew she sounded like a businesswoman, but, she told herself defiantly, that was what she was. "Come and let me show you what I can do for you. I've spent a lot of time working it out."

Mark looked at her a moment longer, as if studying something he couldn't quite understand, couldn't quite grasp in his hand. Then, with a long sigh, he nodded. "Okay. If it'll make you happy, show me."

Chapter 9

THEY WERE QUIET on the short drive to the mill. Sharon had found a rubber band to tie back her hair, and Mark, she noticed gratefully, had managed to tuck in his shirt and button it. She kept the window rolled down. The summer air had turned a little warmer now that it was afternoon, and the fall-like crispness had faded into a softer, moister heat.

Sharon felt numbed by their lovemaking, as though her senses would have to be retaught. She searched for the excitement of the night before and even of this morning, when she had first realized that what Mark wanted —to modernize without losing any jobs—might actually be possible. But the feeling had somehow escaped and then dissipated into nothing, like the steam at the mill.

Maybe she was really crazy, thinking it could be done—or even that Mark really wanted it done. Maybe, she told herself, Mark didn't want to modernize under *any* conditions. Maybe it scared him, having to learn a new system, having to deal with new equipment. She chewed at her lower lip and turned thoughts over in her muddled mind. It was something new to her, a muddled mind. She was used to a mind that clicked away efficiently no matter what the obstacles.

The mill felt relaxed, almost lazy, even though the crew was just as large as it would be on a weekday and the output was just the same. Sharon smiled as she remembered how much she had liked coming with her father when he had worked the afternoon turn on Sundays. Maybe, she thought in retrospect, it was the absence of bosses.

Or maybe I'm just not seeing anything quite right these days.

Mark pulled the little Volkswagen into a parking space and reached over the seat for his hard hat. Sharon suddenly recalled the first day she had arrived here, exactly two weeks ago. Could it possibly have been only fourteen days? It seemed like . . . She laughed. Like another fifteen years, she told herself dryly.

"Where to?" Mark asked. There was a weariness in his voice that touched Sharon's heart.

"I need my hat."

"There's an extra in my car." Mark reached back in and pulled out a cellophane-wrapped, dark-colored hat.

She glanced at it with a smile. "I don't get a white one this time? I'm not management anymore?"

Mark shrugged. "We don't make those kinds of distinctions around here."

"Okay, let's start at the beginning," she said. "The blast furnace. I think . . . Mark . . ." She tried to remember all the details she had worked out the evening before—exactly what would be done to the blast furnace, and where the men would go whose jobs there would be eliminated.

But even before she could begin, the raucous, wailing blast of a siren cut through the air. Suddenly sirens were screaming everywhere, and all sense of laziness disappeared. Men in hard hats were running at top speed, emerging from every shed in the yard, heading for the basic oxygen furnace.

Sharon and Mark had time to exchange one quick glance, and then they were running, too.

Accident. Sharon's brain registered the siren's message at the same moment that her eyes saw the light outside the furnace shed turn red. A matter of seconds, if that. She had time to be grateful as she ran toward the shed that she had on low-heeled shoes and jeans rather than her usual work clothes.

Inside the shed was chaos—people running, sirens splitting the air—but even the chaos was almost lost in the vastness of the dimly lit space. Sharon's eyes searched the darkness for the source of the trouble. She had a sudden vision of her fantasy: dwarves scurrying here and there in the depths of a cave, their movements ordered by some remote, overwhelming giant.

Only this time the giant had made a mistake. Far above them, suspended from the roof beams by its intricate system of cables and hooks, one of the hot-metal ladles was listing dangerously. It was hanging directly over the pulpit, the platform surrounding the furnace itself.

"Mark! It's the ladle!" she cried. "One of the cables has snapped!"

Sharon glanced at the man beside her. Mark's eyes were focused on the ladle, and she could almost see the movements of his mind behind them.

"It won't fall," he said evenly. "The cables will hold it. But it's leaking." He pointed upward, and Sharon could see the small, steady stream of red-hot, liquid metal seeping onto the platform below it. "We gotta get those men off there. There must be enough hot metal on the ground already to cut them off from the stairs, or they would've been down here by now."

For the first time, Sharon saw the four men trapped at the far edge of the pulpit.

"Stay here," Mark ordered without even a glance at Sharon, and then he was off, sprinting toward a group that stood on the ground below the pulpit. As she watched, Sharon saw the men form a knot around him, saw him take the center almost effortlessly and begin to direct whatever rescue operations were being considered.

Sharon stood, her hands clenched at her sides, watching. Mark gestured to the far end of the dark shed, and almost immediately something stirred there, like a giant coming awake. Some massive piece of equipment was being ordered into place. That done, Mark pulled away from the little group and headed up one of the catwalks, toward the pulpit, two steps at a time—to let the trapped men know what was happening, she guessed.

Sharon hated the feeling of helplessness that washed over her as she stood, out of the way. She looked back up at the ladle. Nothing was moving up there. The ladle, the steady stream of molten metal, looked painted against some vast, dark backdrop. After another moment's hesitation, Sharon moved quickly to the catwalks herself. She made her way up the second set of stairs, to the small, brightly lit control booth overlooking the pulpit, where two men sat, silent and still, watching the leak through the glass window.

"What's going on?" she asked briskly. "Any possibility of pulling the ladle back up?"

The men turned to look at her and nodded in recognition. "Can't do a thing," one of them said. "If we move the damn thing, we might have a spill that would eat up whatever space those guys have left."

She looked out the glass pane that separated them from the pulpit, getting her first clear view of the situation there. The four men were sitting on the metal guard-rail at the far end, their feet pulled up, looking self-consciously nonchalant. At their feet, a few yards away, the pool of orange-red liquid reached from one side of the platform to the other and was moving toward the far end. The spread was steady but slow. There was, Sharon told herself, still time. The question was how much.

Sharon pulled a chair up to the television console that showed a schematized picture of the ladle movement. The men in the booth glanced at her quickly, then looked back at their trapped colleagues.

She glanced down at the knot of men on the ground. Mark was back in the middle now, giving orders. She could see his white shirt in the dim light, and the white hard hat that covered his sandy curls. As she watched, he waved at the invisible operator of a huge crane that was now moving across the shed, like some great insect proceeding at slow and stately pace.

I love him. She heard the echo in her mind, and she knew it was absolutely, irretrievably true. *I do love him.* Then, with a sigh, she turned her attention to the control panel in front of her.

It was all familiar; she had worked this sort of panel many times before. "What's the tension on those cables?" she asked.

"You gonna take responsibility?" one of the men asked, a belligerent tinge to his voice.

Sharon looked up at him. "Yes," she said firmly. "I'll take it."

There was a moment when the tension continued, and then suddenly the two men were at her side, ready to help, smiling in relief. It was no longer their problem.

Sharon studied the panel. It wouldn't do, she knew, to look out at the real ladle, the real situation yards away. The screen in front of her told her everything she needed to know, and it let her mind operate free of the emotional tension that watching the men beyond the window would bring.

"Any ideas?" the man to her right asked.

Sharon nodded, her eyes never leaving the screen.

"Two," she said. "We can juggle the tension on those other three cables and try to move it out of there without spilling any more. But I don't know how far we could get it, and it might just go over before we want it to."

"Or?"

"Or we could try to lower it. If we could get a big piece of equipment onto the pulpit, to support the ladle, I might be able to get it down without any more leakage. Then we could replace that cable before we move the ladle across the shed again."

Sharon glanced up. Both men were looking at her with steady gazes.

"You think you could pull one of those off?" one asked softly.

Sharon returned his stare. Then one corner of her mouth rose in a half-smile. "I'm willing to try," she said.

He looked at her a moment longer, as if assessing the possiblilities, then thrust his hand toward her. "I'm Tom. This is Paul over here." He gestured toward the man on her other side. "Anything you want, you just say so."

Sharon shook his extended hand. "I'm Sharon," she said almost shyly. "Thanks."

The second option seemed more controllable; the ladle would remain more or less in position throughout. But it also had the potential for disaster. It would put close to intolerable pressure on the remaining cables as the ladle came down, and it was possible—just possible— that one of them would break. Molten metal would pour out of the ladle like water through a broken dam; injury or even death would be unavoidable.

The control booth was temperature-controlled, but Sharon could feel the heat radiating through the glass panel in front of her. The ladle continued to hang in the air only yards away, and the air around it shimmered with the heat of its load of glowing iron. A drop of perspiration made its slow way down her forehead, settling in one eyebrow, and she raised a hand to wipe her brow, surprised to find a whole line of moisture just at her hairline. Absently, she redid the rubber band that held her hair off her face, her eyes all the time focused on the greenish screen.

She wiped her hands dry on her jeans, then let them fall gently onto the keyboard of the console. The calculations were being made inside her head with a speed and deliberation that almost matched that of the little calculator that lay, unused, to one side. Sharon trusted her brain more than she trusted her fingers not to make mistakes.

"I think we can lay it down on the platform," she said finally, her tone even and firm.

The men glanced across her at each other.

"That's gonna tighten up those cables something fierce."

Sharon nodded. Her eyes remained on the screen, and her fingers now picked out patterns on the keyboard, so that the images changed from figures to a schematic picture of the ladle and its supports, then back to figures.

"I think I can do it," she said again, changing the *we* to an *I*, letting them out of any remaining responsibility for the decision.

Paul shrugged and pushed himself back from the table in front of the window. "I'll tell 'em out there," he said.

Sharon looked up for the first time. "Tell Mark Somers," she said. "He'll know how to handle it. Tell him exactly what I intend to do."

The man looked at her for a moment, then let a faint smile cross his face. He nodded firmly. "You got it, lady. I'll tell 'im."

"Tell him to get those men off the pulpit first, then to clear the area down below. A big area. Tell him to get some heavy equipment on standby. We'll need something to prop up the ladle once I get it down."

"Right."

Sharon barely heard the door shut behind him. Inside the soundproof booth, the only noise was the click of the computer keyboard as she typed in questions, gathering all possible information before she switched to giving the machine instructions. Tom, still in his seat, watched her silently, even his breathing muted by the tension filling the room.

Outside, the four trapped men had balanced on the far railing, their feet pulled up onto the first rung, avoiding the slithering, shallow pool of liquid metal. Sharon glanced out the window at the men and, catching their eye, made a quick thumbs-up sign. But she didn't smile. Behind them she could see the giant crane, almost in place now. She pointed, and the men turned. The rescue itself should be fairly routine. *Those* four men, Sharon told herself, shouldn't have much problem.

Down below, she could see Mark watching the crane, gesturing it into place, and she glimpsed Paul jumping off the last step of the catwalk. He hurried to Mark, and they talked animatedly for a moment. Sharon could see Mark shaking his head vehemently. Then he looked up at the booth.

Sharon smiled. She could see very little except his white hat and shirt in the dim light several stories below, but she knew her face would be clearly visible to him, lit by the fluorescent bulbs of the control booth.

For a brief moment, she thought he was going to come up the catwalks and stop her. He took one tentative step, then turned back to look at the crane. Finally, with one more glance upward, he moved over toward the crane.

Sharon went to work. With a steady tap, she entered instructions into the computer console, telling it precisely what to do, programming it for the movements she wanted. Every now and then she looked up to see what progress had been made in the rescue. On the second or third look, the crane had swung its basket over to within reach of the men, and the first of the four was swinging one leg over the railing.

The stream leaking from the ladle had lessened, as the weight of the metal left inside lightened and the molten ore itself cooled a little. Sharon wanted to make sure whatever she did happened before the metal hardened beyond retrieval; that would ruin the ladle.

She typed in the last set of figures, hesitated a moment, and then stood up. By leaning close to the window, she could see the last of the four men being lowered awkwardly to the ground. The area beneath the pulpit was clear of equipment, and only a handful of people remained below, directing operations. Mark stood at the foot of the catwalks, looking up at the booth, and Sharon gave him a quick thumbs-up sign.

She settled back into her chair and glanced at the man in the seat beside her. "They're going to need all the hands they can find down there to get equipment into place," she said with a nod toward the window. "Maybe you should—"

"They'll do fine," Tom interrupted. "Mark's already got a dozer ready to come up as soon as Red's on the ground. I'll stick with you. You may need help."

Sharon looked at him and smiled. "Right," she said. "Thanks." Then she focused her attention out the window again.

There it was, a huge tractor bulldozer, ready to get lifted into place as soon as the crane was free. Mark was staring up at the booth, obviously waiting for a signal from Sharon that she was ready to start. She could see only shadows where his face was, beneath the rim of his white hat, but she imagined she could see his eyes. She wondered briefly if he were angry with her. He had, after all, told her not to move.

The heat was oppressive. She could feel the dampness on her palms again, and she wiped them roughly on the denim of her jeans. She pulled the red tunic away from her body where it was sticking to her with moisture. Finally she nodded to the other man in the booth.

"Do we have any way of communicating with Mark?" she asked.

Tom moved a few steps to the back of the booth. "Loudspeaker system. We can broadcast, but he can't get back to us."

"Okay. Let's turn it on. Tell him we're ready to go. He should have that thing lifted and ready to swing over as soon as I start the ladle coming down."

Sharon swiveled her chair back to the computer and focused her eyes on the screen. From now on, she told herself, she wouldn't look up, not even once. The figures on the screen were all she needed; she knew that the distraction of the actual ladle, huge and menacing, might sway her perceptions of what needed to be done. Vaguely, as if through a long tunnel, she could hear the man on the loudspeaker talking to Mark, and she could hear the words echoing a split second later outside the booth. She typed in the instruction to begin on the console.

Outside, she knew, the ladle would be starting down. The cables would be playing out, the one diagonal from the broken cable loosened a little, the other two tightened a little. On her screen, a line drawing of the ladle and its cables appeared, and a steady line of figures sped by to one side of it.

Her fingers rested lightly on the keyboard, but the work had really all been done. If she had done it right, in a matter of minutes the ladle would come gently to rest on the platform. If not...

She kept her eyes on the screen, watching for any deviation from what she expected, ready to stop the process if the figures began to indicate too much stress on any of the three remaining cables. But her brain told her that wouldn't happen.

It actually took six minutes for the ladle to reach the pulpit. Sharon felt as if she hadn't breathed during the whole time, and as the figures on her screen abruptly stopped moving, she let herself have the luxury of drawing in one, long deep breath. But it wasn't over.

"Those cables are at their limits," she snapped. "Tell Mark to get the support in there *now*."

"It's already there, Sharon." Tom's voice was soft at the microphone, perfectly attuned to what she needed.

She looked up, away from the screen and, for the first time since the process had begun, out onto the pulpit.

The giant crane was already swinging its cargo, a bulldozer suspended from a magnet four feet in diameter, into place. Then suddenly there was movement on the platform. A handful of hard-hatted men appeared at the top of the catwalk and positioned themselves against the railing, well away from the ladle and out of the way of the bulldozer as it was lowered, but ready to use their weight to push it into place as it swung from its magnet. Mark's white shirt and hard hat were readily identifiable among them. Suddenly Sharon's body, which had seemed entirely without nerve endings for the past twenty minutes, began to quiver.

The tractor was almost in place. It was taking no time at all, but time seemed somehow stopped anyway, suspended in place just as the people around the edges of the shed seemed to be. Sharon heard the door to her booth open and close, and she knew that the man who had stayed with her had gone out to help the men on the pulpit.

Just before he moved to the bulldozer, Mark turned and looked at Sharon through the window. His face was a puzzle of lines and creases, and care and worry showed in his pale blue eyes as clearly as if the emotions were painted there. But suddenly, as though he must have realized how he looked, the worry was replaced with a grin. He winked one eye rakishly at Sharon. Then he turned away.

The cables were holding. The figures on the console in front of Sharon stayed steady. The men put shoulders against the bulldozer where it hung, still a foot or two off the platform, and swung it gently, almost delicately, against the edge of the great ladle. At a signal from Mark, the crane operator lowered the magnet the remaining eighteen inches, and the support was in place. Sharon took a deep breath and let it out slowly, then rested her head back against the chair and closed her eyes.

Beyond the soundproof booth, there was a faint roar as the people on the floor cheered. Behind her, Sharon heard the door to the booth open and close softly.

Fingers touched her shoulders, then the back of her neck. She opened her eyes. Mark stood behind her, his strong hands gently removing the rubber band that pulled her hair tautly away from her face, gently massaging the back of her head as her hair fell loose about her shoulders. Sharon looked up at his upside-down face.

His eyes with their long, sand-colored lashes had narrow circles of red all around them, and there was a streak of grease across one cheek. Slowly, he lowered his face toward hers, and Sharon gratefully felt the soft touch of his mouth against her own. But as they kissed, she could taste the sickly sweet hint of blood.

She sat up. "Mark?" She swiveled the chair around abruptly to face him. "Are you hurt? Did something happen?"

He was grinning the familiar grin. "You do that with that chair again and I'll be crippled for life. *Never* be able to father a child."

Sharon took his hands in hers again and studied his face. There was a thin line of blood running from his hairline down to his cheek, along his left eye. Mark wiped at it ineffectually with one hand.

"I turned around too fast by the dozer. Somebody was pushing the other way. It'll heal just fine."

Tenderly, Sharon pulled his face to her and touched her lips to the cut. She could feel heat radiating from it, and the edges looked dangerously raw. Mark leaned over and kissed the top of her head.

Sharon was suddenly aware of the activity outside the booth, just beyond the glass panel. Asbestos-suited men had already disengaged the broken cable from its hook, and what was left of it had been rewound. A new cable was being strung already. In a matter of minutes, it would be attached and the ladle would be ready to go again. In time.

Immediately beyond the window, the two men who had shared the booth with Sharon were standing, looking in with huge grins on their faces.

Sharon dropped Mark's hands abruptly. "Mark," she whispered, "everyone can see!"

He looked at her and grinned. "Ah, so they can," he whispered back. "But you know what? I don't give a damn!" His voice was louder, almost shouting. "We're all safe, the whole damn place, and you did it! I'm so proud of you, Sharon Dysart!"

He slid his hands under her arms and pulled her up out of her chair. Sharon felt her legs buckle slightly and then steady, and she put her arms around his waist and held herself against him. They stood that way, comforting each other with their bodies, for a long moment before Sharon stepped back.

"Mark, do the rest of the yards know what's going on here? And we need to fire up the reserve basic oxygen furnace."

Mark shook his head, grinning his lopsided grin. "That little mind just keeps clicking away, doesn't it? Yes, everyone knows. The fire department is on its way, just in case. An ambulance is outside. Two guys were hurt, and they're already out there. Burns. But I haven't got the other furnace started up yet. Thought I'd breathe first."

Suddenly Sharon felt her legs buckle again, and this time they refused to steady. She crumpled against the chair behind her. Mark knelt in front of her at once, taking her hands in his, his face close to hers.

"Sharon! Love! Are you all right?" Then he stood up resolutely. "Come on. I'm taking you home."

Sharon shook her head insistently. "No, really, I'm fine. We need to make sure everything's okay."

"Everything's just fine, except you. For once let me take care of you, okay?"

"But your face..."

Mark grimaced at her fiercely and pulled her to her feet. As he led her out of the little control booth, his arm around her shaking shoulders, Sharon felt a wave of heat against her face, almost as if someone had thrown a hot, wet towel at her. She stumbled slightly, and Mark caught her arm. Despite the extraordinary heat, her teeth were chattering.

The pulpit was crowded with men now, but the crowds parted as Mark led her forward, and all eyes followed them. The faces of the men were curious but friendly, and full of something that Sharon, when she thought about it later, could identify only as respect. She had saved them time and money and maybe lives, and they knew it. She smiled wanly as Mark led her by them.

He guided her down the narrow grated stairs and through the dim cavern of the shed. Outside the sun was so bright that she instinctively raised a hand to shield her eyes. Mark kept one arm wrapped around her shoulders. With the other hand, he held her elbow and led her carefully toward the battered Volkswagen.

Sharon was beginning to feel silly. After all, she hadn't suffered any injuries. It was only the aftermath of tension she was feeling. But the pressure of Mark's arm around her shoulder was so pleasant that she didn't really want him to take it away.

"Wait here a minute. I gotta get something on this cut," he said as they reached the battered Volkswagen. Sharon leaned against it and watched him lope gracefully toward the white ambulance that stood just beside the entrance to the shed. When his tall figure disappeared around the other side of it, she felt a tiny pang of loss, then smiled at her own silliness.

"I'm . . . I'm really okay, Mark. You need to do things here," she said when he returned only moments later, a streak of red antiseptic down one side of his face. But even she could hear how weak her voice sounded. "There's absolutely nothing wrong with me," she said more firmly.

"Uh-huh." He hunted in his pocket for the car keys.

"Mark, you have responsibilities." Sharon straightened her shoulders as he took her elbow and opened the car door. "I can get a cab back to the inn."

"Shut up, Sharon," he said, hardly looking at her. "Stop being your usual bully. Just get in the car."

Sharon opened her mouth, then snapped it shut. She glared at him as he folded her into the front seat of the Volkswagen. But when he had slid in under the steering wheel himself, he turned and looked at her. He was smiling, but the smile was tender and vulnerable.

"Sharon, please. Let somebody else worry about the responsibilities this once. Let me be in love with you, just this once. Without anything else interfering."

Sharon stared at him, and his pale blue eyes glowed back at her. There was that word again. Love. *Let me be in love with you*. Somewhere deep inside, in the very center of her, the low fire began to burn higher again. When have I ever stopped you? she thought giddily to herself.

Then she smiled at him. "Okay," she said in a small voice. He leaned over and kissed her gently on the mouth, then turned the key and started the engine.

Sharon let her head fall back against the seat and

closed her eyes, as she had in the control booth. She had a vague sense that they were climbing too sharply to be returning to Mark's Otawnee apartment. But she wasn't really thinking about anything at all except Mark's words.

It took her by surprise when Mark pulled into the driveway of the great stone mansion by the park and stopped the car.

"Here we are," he announced.

Sharon opened her eyes wide. "Mark, this is your *father's* house."

Mark shrugged. "I used to live here, too, you know. And they tell me I'm welcome back anytime. Besides . . ." He shifted in the seat to face her and winked. "The folks are off in Pittsburgh for the weekend. Won't be back until morning."

He led her quickly through the front of the house, and Sharon barely had time to register what it looked like. Formal, lovely, it was decorated in fashionable shades of mauve and cream. The perfect backdrop, she thought dryly, for Byron and Charlotte Somers's elegance.

The room they finally entered, at the end of a long corridor, was so obviously the bedroom of a high school boy that Sharon almost giggled. Trophies and books competed for room on the shelves, and several tennis racquets were stacked in one corner. The bed was large, with a dark brown spread, and a desk sat against one wall. There was even a Monet print hanging over the bed; Sharon recognized it as the same one that had hung over her own.

She shook her head with a little laugh. "Mark," she began.

"Get undressed," he said. "I'll start the water running in the tub."

He disappeared for a moment, and Sharon heard the sound of a bathtub filling. She stood in the center of the room, looking around, drinking in Mark as a teenager, trying to form another image of him from his possessions.

"Sharon," he said slightly petulantly when he returned. "I said, get undressed."

Sharon looked at him. "Yes, sir, right away, sir."

Mark stuck his tongue out at her, then smiled. "Be right back," he said, and headed out of the bedroom again into the hall.

Alone, Sharon slipped out of her jeans and pulled the tunic off over her head. It was almost soaking from perspiration. She went into the bathroom and piled her clothes neatly on a little footstool next to the tub. The tub itself was huge and square, with several faucets Sharon recognized as whirlpool controls. She was too tired to be surprised; she felt only gratitude at the sensual delights that apparently awaited her.

Carefully, she lowered her tense body into the hot water and flipped her hair back over the edge of the tub, then leaned her head back against the comfortably slanted side. It felt wonderful.

Chapter 10

SHARON OPENED HER eyes at the sound of the door opening and closing again.

"Hi, love. Feeling better?" Mark stood beside the tub, wrapped in a long, dark blue terry-cloth robe.

Sharon nodded slowly, a satisfied smile playing at her mouth. "Mmm. I was really tense."

"And no wonder. Wonder Woman rescues an entire steel mill."

"Not quite, Mark. Only a basic oxygen furnace."

Mark put a finger to the side of his nose. "Ah. In any case, we have just the thing for tension." He leaned over the tub and fiddled with the faucets, and Sharon felt a sudden surge of pressure against her lower back and legs.

"Whoo!" She shivered slightly as her body registered the pleasure of it. "Not bad. Did you have this little toy in high school?"

Mark nodded. "Some doctor friend of my parents told them athletes needed whirlpool baths. Even kid athletes. So they bought one. Nothing too good for little Markie, of course."

"Must have been nice," Sharon said softly, closing her eyes as the water surged around her, drawing the tension out of her muscles.

"Still is. Can I get in now?"

Sharon rolled over onto her side. The water pushed against her breasts, caressing them. "Just give me one more minute," she said. "It feels so nice."

"Welcome to it," he answered, turning his back on her. "But I'm coming in anyway. I worked hard, too, you know, and besides, I'm wounded."

In one quick motion he had stripped off his robe and stepped into the tub, sliding into the corner opposite Sharon. Their legs were a jumble in the center of the bath, and Sharon, with a giggle, tried to extricate hers and pull them to one side. But Mark caught them between his knees.

"No need," he said casually. "There's plenty of room." He grinned and raised one eyebrow in a leer. "Plenty of room," he repeated.

He reached for Sharon and pulled himself around to her side of the tub. His movements set up a responsive movement in the water; little waves rippled across the surface and splashed against the side. Sharon slithered away, but he wrapped one strong arm around her and pulled her back.

"And to think," he murmured, his mouth against her ear, "I lived with this tub for ten years and never realized its potential."

He held her against him. Sharon's body throbbed with the pleasure of touching him, and with the feel of the water pulsating all around them, touching every part of her body. He buried his face against her throat and nuzzled it with his lips.

"You were astonishing today, love," he said softly.

Sharon kissed his tangled, sweat-soaked hair. "I know my stuff," she said. "Thanks for trusting me to do it right. Now if you'd only trust me to do the rest of my job..."

Mark sank down under the water, head and all, until only his face remained above the surface. *"Please,* no business!" He opened his eyes and looked at her slyly, and Sharon suddenly felt an additional pressure at the inside of her thighs, something that wasn't just the water jets.

"Oh, Mark..."

Mark pulled himself up again. "Promise," he said. "Promise, no more business." His hand was insistent now, adding its strong pressure to the rhythmic pulsating of the water. "Come on, Sharon, promise."

Sharon could feel her body responding to the caresses; she could feel the answering movements begin deep inside her. "That's not fair, Mark," she murmured, hardly aware of what she was saying.

He held one of her breasts in his other hand and brought his mouth to it, flicking his tongue across the already wet, erect tip. "Come on," he repeated lazily.

Sharon groaned and shifted her body toward him, wrapping her arms and legs around him, covering him as surely as the water covered them both. "I promise," she whispered hoarsely.

Their bodies moved together with the rhythm of the water, and suddenly the insistent pressure between her legs became stronger, harsher, and the pressure of the water against every limb and nerve was no longer separable from the pressures of Mark's hands and of his male strength, and she could no longer tell what she was feeling inside and what she was feeling outside. Then a pulsing heat shot through her whole body with such violence that she shuddered in response, and water splashed against the sides of the tub and over the edges.

Finally, the rhythms began to subside and their bodies quieted. Sharon lay back against the side of the tub again, letting the water lap gently over her, and Mark sat up and fiddled with the faucets. The movement in the water stopped, and the huge, square tub was just a bathtub again.

He looked at her through half-closed eyes, his pleasure gleaming out at her from the pale blue. Sharon took a deep breath. She smiled back at him.

"You look like a real war casualty," she said laughingly. "That stuff they put on your cut is running down the side of your face."

Mark reached a hand to it and wiped at it. Sharon pushed herself up and reached for a washcloth.

"Bath time," she said, as lightly as she could manage. The intensity of what they had just shared still possessed her.

She gently cleaned the cut on his face, then went to work on his smooth, muscular body with the soapy cloth, rubbing his legs and arms, his broad chest with its line of reddish curls, his neck, behind his ears. Mark emitted funny little moans of pleasure as she worked, shifting his body now and then to let her reach out-of-the-way places.

"Okay," she said finally. "All done. Just your hair."

With a quick, strong motion, she dunked his head under the water. He came up sputtering and reaching for her, and she barely had time to grab hold of her nose before she was under water. When Mark let her up, her hair hung in ropes over her shoulders, black and glistening. He was grinning, as usual.

They sat cross-legged in the tub and washed each other's hair. Sharon luxuriated in the feel of his strong, gentle hands against her scalp, and the horrors and tensions of only an hour earlier were almost forgotten.

Suddenly Mark raised his head and sniffed the air.

"Tea," he said cheerfully. "Another nice thing about being rich: You ask for things, and they appear."

He stood up. Sharon watched admiringly as his athlete's body rose from the tub, water cascading off it and catching the light, making the planes and sinews of it gleam.

He held his hands down to her and pulled her to her feet, then reached for two towels from a nearby shelf and handed one to Sharon. His own he used with quick, deliberate strokes, then wrapped around his waist like a sarong.

Sharon rubbed herself dry slowly. Her skin felt alive to every sensation, and the towel was soft against it.

Mark was already in the bedroom when she was dry, so she wrapped herself in the big, blue robe he had worn earlier, lost herself in its bigness, and found a smaller towel to wrap around her wet hair. It was wonderful to have all the grime and memories of the accident washed away.

A tray sat on the desk in the bedroom with a steaming pot of tea and a napkin-covered basket.

"Mmmm," Mark said, pulling the napkin off and leaning over the tray. "Blueberry muffins."

Sharon's eyebrows rose a little. Was there really a lifestyle that involved fresh blueberry muffins at twenty minutes' notice? When she had been married to Jean-Paul, the meals had been elegant and excellent, provided by a slightly temperamental cook who had finally quit in the midst of the divorce battles. And since then she had lived more or less alone, with the help of a regular cleaning woman in her modern New York apartment. Most of her time had been spent in hotels. But this, fresh muffins on call . . .

"What a pleasant way to live," she said, amused.

Mark looked up at her. "You keep saying that," he said thoughtfully. Then he straightened up and smiled. "I feel good about living in Otawnee, in that apartment, but I do have my moments when I miss the old shack."

"Maybe," Sharon began tentatively, "maybe there *is* something in between. Maybe a house..."

He looked at her. "With a yard..."

"Halfway down the hill..."

"Kids..." He was looking at her with widened eyes, and Sharon nervously shifted her gaze to the muffins.

"Well," she said, "food." She settled into a chair and poured herself a cup of tea. She had had doughnuts and coffee at eleven, and it was now almost four. She pulled two muffins onto a plate and buttered them with quick, efficient motions.

"Hungry?" Mark asked sarcastically. He watched her as he pulled on jeans and a knit polo shirt. "Do you think I could get one, too?"

Sharon, her mouth full of muffin, buttered another and handed it to Mark. She felt a little twinge of regret at the disappearance of his smooth, tan chest beneath the dark green shirt.

"You know, Sharon," he said thoughtfully, pulling another chair up to the desk beside hers, "you really were wonderful with that control panel. I think you know more about that equipment than I do."

Sharon's eyes widened. "Of course I do," she said with a twinge of annoyance. "That's my job. I'm good at it." She looked at him levelly as she continued, "And if you put in the stuff I'm going to recommend, you'll never have that kind of accident again."

Mark leaned back in his chair, closed his eyes, and groaned. "I can't believe this. We've just been through hell together and..." He paused and opened his eyes for a moment, then closed them again. "And a little bit of heaven, too, of course. I'm impressed. You're good at what you do. Now let's just forget about it for a day."

Sharon took another sip of tea. "It's part of what we're all about, Mark. What I do. The point is, if you really care about your work force the way you say you do—"

Mark sat up straight in his chair and opened his eyes, staring steadily at Sharon. "Don't you believe I do?" he asked, interrupting.

Sharon nodded impatiently. "Of course. That's what I'm trying to say. *Since* you really care about your work force, you want them working with safe equipment, right? So just listen to what I'm thinking about."

"What I want is a work force precisely as large as the one I've got now." He leaned toward her with a lopsided smile and put a hand playfully over her mouth. "Tell you what, Sharon. Marry me. Then we can fight in peace. You can play the stock market to your heart's content, and run those shares of Lacombe Industries as high as you want. At least then you wouldn't be playing with live bodies."

"Mark, if you'd just—" Sharon stopped abruptly as what Mark had just said sank in. "Marry you?" she repeated dumbly. She felt cloudy, as if reality had suddenly become obscured and she couldn't quite tell what was from what wasn't. "Marry you? That's not . . ." She swallowed hard and blinked. "That's not funny, Mark."

"It's not meant to be. It's the only way I know to shut you up."

The temptation was almost overwhelming to shout *yes,* to shout it as loud as she could. Marry Mark Somers! It would be . . . not just the fulfillment of her earliest dreams, but the fulfillment of her very grown-up desires. I love him, she thought.

But there was still one more battle to be fought. He had to be willing to listen to her. Without that, she would never know—never know if this was just another, even more drastic way of buying her off; never know if she was still a trophy for him, a symbol of how far he had moved from his roots.

She scrambled for something to say to fill the silence. "I'm beginning to think you're just scared, Mark.

You've paid what you consider your family's dues, and now you're scared you'll have to start all over again, learn the steel business all over again." She cleared her throat and straightened her shoulders. "I think you're scared the... the *romance* will go out of it. The giants and dwarves working away in their dark caverns."

Mark rolled his eyes toward the ceiling. "What *is* this? I'm asking you to marry me here, and I get back some insanity about being scared and about giants and—" He looked back at her suddenly through narrowed eyes. His hands were jammed in his pockets, as though he was keeping them there by an effort of will.

"Wait a minute," he said. "Those are *your* fantasies, love." His brow knit into a frown as he looked at her. "Is that what all this is about? I get rid of my past by living in Otawnee and working at the mill like a hand. Maybe you get rid of yours by deliberately destroying all those romantic fantasies, all those things you felt when you were a child. You actually chose to do that for a living, to erase all those fantasies, like a penance for having actually enjoyed something when you were a kid."

He leaned forward again and put both hands on her shoulders. His face was so close Sharon could see the little scar on his nose again, and the thin scarlet line down the side of his face looked raw. "Don't do it, Sharon. Don't banish the romance from your soul."

His mouth felt wonderfully warm against hers, and it tasted of blueberries and butter and spicy herb tea.

"If you'll just listen," she murmured, trying to escape from his embrace. But he only pulled her closer.

"Tell me tomorrow," he said softly.

It would be so simple, Sharon thought, to do exactly what he says for the rest of my life.

But she pushed her chair back and broke away from his touch. "Okay," she said, defiance making her voice a little louder than usual. "This once, I'll do exactly what

I'm told. I'm supposed to give a preliminary presentation tomorrow at the lunch meeting anyway. I assume you'll attend?"

She looked at him questioningly, and he nodded.

Mark watched her as she gathered her clothes and disappeared into the bathroom to get dressed. He was still sitting in his chair, his hands once again jammed into his pockets, when she returned in her jeans and tunic, her hair brushed into one long, wet tumble.

"Thanks for everything, Mark. The bath, the food, the . . ." She paused, uncomfortable, then heard herself giggle a little. "Everything," she finished weakly.

He shrugged. "Only the best for the lady who saved the mill," he said. The expression on his face was inscrutable, as though he was willing himself to show nothing at all.

"My car is over in Otawnee," Sharon went on. "Maybe you could give me a lift?"

Mark nodded slowly, still watching her. "If I promise to listen tomorrow, will you promise to answer me?"

Sharon looked at him curiously. "Answer you?" she asked.

"About marrying me."

Sharon opened her mouth and then shut it again. She played with the car keys she had pulled out of her back pocket.

Mark let out a long breath. "Okay," he said. "Let's go."

They were both quiet on the way back down the hill and across the bridge. Sharon gave brief, businesslike directions to the old house. As they pulled up in front, Mark peered out the windshield with interest.

"I remember this house," he said. "Except then it was white, wasn't it?"

He gestured at the pale green paint that was peeling here and there.

Sharon nodded. "I can't imagine you remember it," she said. "It looks exactly like every other house on this block. In this neighborhood, for that matter."

"That's why I remember it," he said. "I remember being afraid that you'd turn out to live somewhere ...different. I loved that your house was just like the next one, which was just like the next one..."

Sharon looked at him sharply. "Mark, did anyone ever tell you how truly weird you are?" she asked. Then, with a quick smile, she pushed the door open and was out of the car.

The little boy was still playing in the yard.

"Watched your car for ya," he called, running toward Sharon as she moved down the sidewalk.

She looked at him and smiled, then reached for her purse. "Let me give you something for your trouble," she said.

He stopped and looked down at the sidewalk.

"Not allowed to take anything from other folks," he said softly.

Sharon studied his small form for a moment, recognizing the pride that kept his shoulders stiff. She had looked that way herself for many years.

"I'm not 'other folks,'" she answered finally. "I used to live in your house. It's like I'm part of the family." She pulled a couple of dollar bills from her purse and stuffed them into his pocket. "You tell your mom it's okay."

He glanced up at her shyly and nodded. "Thank you, ma'am," he said. With a quick look at the man who sat in the little car still parked by the curb, he turned and disappeared into the house.

Sharon climbed into her own car and started the engine. She raised her eyes to the rearview mirror. Mark was still there, watching, making sure she was all right. The love she felt for him flooded her body with warmth.

She waved once, then put her foot on the accelerator and drove off.

By meeting time the next day, Sharon felt as if her whole body were made up of nerve endings. She had spent the evening going over and over her figures, trying to find any possible discrepancies, and trying to decide how to make the presentation.

There were two plans. The first, the more conventional, would involve fairly substantial layoffs, but it would also improve the profit line. She knew that from eight years of experience, and she could guarantee it. Layoffs coupled with substantial investments in new equipment would do the job.

The plan she had worked on for the last two days, the one that took all of Mark Somers's objections into consideration, was more risky. True, she thought she could account for every job, could find a new slot for everyone in training programs. And the equipment investment would be slightly less, to offset the additional labor costs. If it worked, it would be a real coup for SomerSteel and for Dysart, Inc. It would be the kind of plan that plants with labor and union problems desperately needed. *If* it worked. But that was the sticky point: She couldn't guarantee the result.

She was still unsure whether to present both plans and let the officers of SomerSteel decide, or to present only the second plan, and to sell it with all the skills available to her.

She pushed open the door to the conference room with a sigh. What I really need, she told herself, is the time to experiment with it. If I could just stay on here for a few months, see how it works, fiddle with it when something doesn't go the way I've expected. *That* would be perfect.

The buffet table was in place, exactly where it had

been the week before and the week before that, and most of the officers were already at their seats, plates of food and cups of coffee in front of them. Byron Somers greeted Sharon with a big smile.

"I hear you got another ride home from the dance the other night," he said cheerfully.

Sharon felt the warmth of embarrassment touch her cheeks. She had almost forgotten the dance, three short evenings ago. "Why yes," she said, determined not to give in to emotions. "Mark was kind enough to take me home. We had some business to discuss."

Byron nodded, still smiling, and for the first time Sharon could see in his smile a more controlled version of Mark's wide, off-center grin. "Glad to hear you and Mark are getting along," he said, giving her arm a little pat. "I also hear you did quite a job for us here yesterday. Saved us a great deal of trouble."

Sharon smiled back at him. "All in the line of duty," she said lightly.

He nodded. "Well, I'm eager to hear what you have to tell us. Do have some food." He turned away to talk to someone else almost before he had finished the sentence.

Sharon watched his back for a moment before she moved to the buffet table. It was remarkable. His plant had suffered a serious accident just twenty-four hours earlier, and all he could say was "Have some food." She shook her head in disbelief. Not that he wasn't concerned; she was sure he'd been in touch with the hospital to check on the injured men, and with their families, to see if there was anything he could do for them. But there was something refreshing, in contrast, about Mark's earnest intensity.

Sharon felt unexpectedly hungry, and she piled the cold cuts and salads high on her plate. As she slipped into her seat, Mark came into the room. He was dressed, as he had been two weeks before, in cords and a work shirt, and he was deep in conversation with one of the other officers. He looked curiously incongruous amidst the three-piece suits.

Byron dispensed with the routine business, then turned to Sharon. "Well, Miss Dysart, we wish to express our appreciation for your actions yesterday. We have all heard that without your expertise, the damage might have been much greater."

Sharon dipped her head in acknowledgment and glanced at Mark. His head was down, studying his hands.

"And you have, I think, a preliminary report for us."

Sharon looked at the pile of print-outs in front of her. She glanced from Byron to Mark, and then back again, and suddenly she pulled the original modernization plan off the top of the pile and slipped it underneath. She stared at the top sheet now in front of her.

"Yes," she said firmly. "I have some things to say that I think might interest you very much." She swung her glance around to Mark, seated at the other end of the table. His eyes gleamed at her, and she could feel the tiny tingling she had felt the first moment she had seen him, late at night, in the mill yard. She cleared her throat.

"It is always my intention," she began, "wherever I work, to balance efficiency with humanity. That is, without putting too many people out of work. However, in the past, that has always seemed to me an inevitable part of the modernization process. As higher degrees of technology are put in place, labor-intensive areas are phased out."

She glanced at Mark again. He was leaning back in his chair, his eyes focused on the ceiling. It almost seemed as if he wasn't listening. Resolutely, Sharon went on.

"But what I've seen here at SomerSteel was a challenge. This is an area where unemployment is already way out of bounds. Steel is an industry where the future looks rather bleak, for labor as well as for management. SomerSteel is a small, profitable operation, one that is already in rather good shape."

She nodded at Mark. He was looking at her now, his face a blank page. He returned her nod.

"There is no doubt that certain jobs will be eliminated if you move to the kind of operation I expect to recommend for you—continuous casting, computerization, some robotics. The mill will be safer for everyone."

Mark had sunk a little in his chair. He had, she knew, heard this much before, and he was not impressed. She pulled one sheet of paper aside and looked at the one beneath it for a moment.

"But what I've done here that is different and, for me, exciting," she went on, looking intently at the paper in front of her, "is to draft a plan for retraining those workers whose jobs will be eliminated." She folded her hands over the papers in front of her and looked at Mark, steadily, defiantly. "All of them."

Mark was still leaning back in his chair, but now he returned her gaze, his eyes lazy and half-closed.

"I would like to see people trained to do a variety of jobs, so they are not limited to any one part of the mill. I would like to see a technological training program. Many of these men can be moved easily into more creative and demanding positions—the kind that modernization will provide."

Sharon could hear the excitement in her own voice as she sketched her plans. It *could* work, she knew it could. And it would be fun to stay with it, to watch it work.

"What about costs?" Byron Somers broke into her outline with forceful vigor. "I thought that was the point of all this: to increase productivity and profits."

Sharon looked at him. His brow was knit into a frown. She was, she realized, moving too fast for Byron.

She smiled. "Of course. I'm sorry. There will be

minimal extra costs in salaries and setting up training programs, but my figures show that these will be more than offset by increased profit margins on higher productivity. I'll be honest with you. I've—I've never tried to implement this kind of a plan before, Mr. Somers."

She leaned toward Byron, using all the ammunition she had accumulated over eight years of negotiating with mill owners. "My preliminary figures show that it could work. I can't deny there would be some risk. No one has ever tried quite this kind of program before. But if we can pull it off—and I want to emphasize that before I recommend anything concrete, I will be able to show you every single projected calculation—SomerSteel will be famous as an innovative, humane, and *profitable* corporation."

Sharon's full attention was focused on Byron Somers; all she could think of in the world at that moment was winning him over to her plan. She had almost forgotten Mark existed.

Byron looked interested but skeptical. "I don't know, Sharon," he began. "If it's never been tried—"

"I think Ms. Dysart is proposing some extraordinary changes," Mark broke in. Sharon jerked upright in her chair, as though someone had pulled strings attached to her shoulders. She wanted to turn and look at him, but she couldn't make herself do it. Her eyes remained on Byron.

She sensed rather than saw Mark rise from his chair; she could almost feel the heat his body generated in the closed room.

"Most of you know, I've been opposed to modernization down the line," he went on. "Because it would eliminate jobs. I could never agree to the loss of jobs."

Sharon studied the paper in front of her. Her hands, she saw to her surprise, were absolutely steady. She had done her job well; she had convinced a boss. And she had only been here two weeks. She smiled dryly to herself. As if that was all she really cared about at this point.

"I'm not absolutely convinced Ms. Dysart can pull it off—institute her plan without any loss of jobs at all," Mark said.

Sharon felt a little frown knit her brow. So she hadn't talked him into it. Her eyes stayed steady on the stack of papers. She reached for her cup of now-cooled coffee.

"If you'd care to look over my figures, Mark—" she began, but he was talking again.

"The only way it seems possible," he said, "is if she and I work closely together on this. I think, between the two of us, we *can* make these plans operational without losing a single man. Or woman," he added, and suddenly his voice sounded different, amused.

Sharon looked up at him for the first time. He was standing beside his chair at the end of the table, looking at her with his sparkling, pale blue eyes. The overhead lights shot glints of yellow through his sandy curls, and small shadows played beneath his eyes and nose and outlined his high cheekbones. The cut on his cheek was now a thin line of darker brown against his tan face. And his body . . . ah, his body!

But best of all was the smile playing around the corners of his mouth, as if he wanted to grin but was preventing himself by sheer brute control of the muscles of his face. Sharon blinked. It was not the expression she had expected to see.

"The thing is," Mark went on, stroking his chin in his best businessman manner, "we'll need someone here for a much longer time than Ms. Dysart is contracted to stay. Here at the mill to oversee all this. Someone who can balance my perspective on all this, keep me on track." He was pacing beside the table now, and the eyes of everyone at it followed his movements. "I'd like to propose that we hire Ms. Dysart to do that job."

He stopped abruptly beside Sharon. "That is, if she'll have it."

Sharon's mouth fell open, and she snapped it shut.

When she remained silent, Mark spoke one more time. "I'd also like to propose..." he said. "Well..."

At last he let the grin break through, and Sharon felt as if the sun had burst from behind a cloud. "Hell, I'd just like to propose. Once again. Making up for fifteen lost years."

The eyes of all those around the table shifted suddenly to Sharon, and she knew she was blushing a bright red. She swallowed hard, reaching for her voice, but it refused to come.

He trusted her plan! And he was serious! About marriage *and* about the work she could do here. It was a fantasy too good to be true. But it *was* true. And this time, this time she would not refuse it.

She smiled directly at Mark, as if no one else in the room existed. She could hear throats being discreetly cleared all around, but it didn't matter. Professionalism, self-discipline, everything she had thought she valued most deeply fell before her overwhelming desire to give Mark an answer.

"Oh, yes!" she cried finally, and he collapsed in a mock faint, holding on to the back of her chair. "Oh, yes," she said again, more softly, shifting in her chair to face him.

He wiped his brow. "Good thing," he said. "Where else could I find a woman who'd go parking with me just to get a better view of the thirty-six-inch mill?"

Sharon and Mark sat cross-legged on the grass, eating barbecued chicken and licking the sweet, spicy sauce off their fingers. Byron Somers had given out the candy and balloons, and had even been persuaded to join the volleyball game. Mark and Sharon had led opposing teams in the sack race—Otawnee versus Somerville—and the result was still being hotly disputed by Harry Prysovich and a colleague from across the river.

The sun sent golden glints through Mark's tangled hair.

They had been silent for some minutes.

"What made it happen, Mark?" Sharon said finally, thoughtfully.

Mark looked at her questioningly. "What made *what* happen? There was only you to get to agree. I'd already proposed."

Sharon smiled and shook her head. "No, I mean what finally convinced you that modernization would work at SomerSteel? The way you wanted it to?"

Mark's eyes widened. "You *said* it would. What else did I need?"

"But I'd been saying I could do it right from the start. You wouldn't listen until that meeting."

He knit his brow into a little frown. Behind his aviator sunglasses, Sharon could just make out the sparkle of his light eyes.

"Yeah," he agreed thoughtfully. "But that meeting was the first time you said you weren't sure. Before that you'd been so damned positive." He looked at her and grinned, and it was like the first time all over again. Sharon's fingers tingled, and she felt the little flames begin in the base of her belly. "I finally felt like maybe I could have something to say in the whole process. I kind of liked that feeling. I like my lady to have a few doubts now and then."

Sharon picked up his hand and licked the fingertips, then leaned forward and kissed him hard on the mouth.

"And I like my man to like his job. *And* his lady. And *her* job." She rocked back onto the grass and smiled. "It's always been one of my favorite fantasies."

All of the above titles are $1.95
Prices may be slightly higher in Canada.

HERE'S WHAT READERS ARE SAYING ABOUT

Second Chance at Love ®

"I think your books are great. I love to read them as does my family."
— *P. S., Milford, MA**

"Your books are some of the best romances I've read."
— *M. B., Zeeland, MI**

"SECOND CHANCE AT LOVE is my favorite line of romance novels."
— *L. B., Springfield, VA**

"I think SECOND CHANCE AT LOVE books are terrific. I married my 'Second Chance' over 15 years ago. I truly believe love is lovelier the second time around!"
— *P. P., Houston, TX**

"I enjoy your books tremendously."
— *I. S., Bayonne, NJ**

"I love your books and read them all the time. Keep them coming—they're just great."
— *G. L., Brookfield, CT**

"SECOND CHANCE AT LOVE books are definitely the best!"
— *D. P., Wabash, IN**

*Name and address available upon request